1秒開口說英語

好流利！用動詞溜英語

附 MP3

與金錢的生死時速

施孝昌◎著

[前言]

活用 52 個動詞，1 秒流利說英語

1 秒流利說英語，秘訣是：活用 52 個「動詞」，你的英語會立刻「動」起來。面對老外，對答如流，老外怎麼說，都聽得懂。

這 52 個「動詞」，都是老外天天用、最常用的動詞。善用它，你的英語會話超「動感」。說英語，其實很簡單！Basic Verbs for Everyday English.，讓你美夢成真，你只要會用幾個最簡單、最常用，又具有「動感」的單字，你的英語就能說的很「跳」、很「活」！

身在國際化時代，不會英語真是寸步難行、有口難言；會英語，晉升、求職都能高人一等。

在學習英語的過程中，最令我們感到頭痛的，可能就是動詞的部份了，因為這個部份既深廣又難。

本書精選 52 個最常用的動詞，把最深奧的動詞部份，用最簡單淺顯的重點方式，分析解說，並加以活用，讓您迅速掌握英語的學習核心。

只用幾個最簡易、好用、有含意又具有「動感」的單字，保證你就能把英語說得很溜、很活，克服語言障礙，讓人刮目相看。

一般人學習英語十幾年，還不會應用，不敢開口，本書讓您重建信心，把英語說得和母語一樣好，語言生動活潑，在短期內發揮十足潛力，一舉成功。

如此一來，無論考試、求職、晉升或與老外聊天，您都可以行遍天下無敵手，溝通無國界。

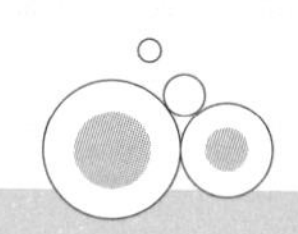

目錄

CONTENTS

CONTENTS

>>> 1 <<<

go

文法特強調

說英語，其實很簡單！你只要會用幾個最簡單、最常用、又具有「動感」的單字，你的英語就能說的很「跳」，很活！像 go，只有兩個字母而已，誰不會？但 go 卻是最跳的一個字。一般學校裡只教你用 go to school, go home，真是天大的可惜啊！

go 的精髓不在 go to school, go home，而在顯示由 A 點到 B 點中間的「過、過、過…程」，它是在動的，你一定要感覺出來這種表示「經過」的動感！所以，凡事從一種狀態變到另一種狀態，你都可以用 go 來表達，例如：牛奶放久了、壞了，你可以說 It goes bad.，你看，你把牛奶從新鮮到變壞的過程，這樣簡單就描述出來了！不僅是牛奶，所有的事物從好變壞都可以說是 go....bad。

go 的過去式是 went，所以，如果您要強調牛奶或某個東西在過去的「那時」就變壞了，你就說 It went bad.

go 還有一種變形，一般英文法稱為「過去分詞」，也就是 gone 的形式，gone 通常與 is、was、am、has、have 這類的所謂 be 動詞、助動詞一起使用。這個字好用得很！ gone 的意思仍是表示從一點到另一點的變化與過程，但它強調那個過程已經完成了，不能再變了。有了這樣的含意，使用起來就可以讓你的英語很漂亮。例如你下班，要回家了，就對還在苦幹的同事們宣布：Adios!（西班牙語：再見），I am gone.，意思是：「各位苦命的同志，你們繼續努力吧，本人要落跑了，不能陪你們衝衝衝了！」還有，你早已計畫好要去度假，老闆臨時說，「慢著，你得來加班趕工！」，你只能嘆息說，My vacation is gone. 意思是：「我的假期，飛了！」凡事是煮熟的鴨子飛了，東西本來好好的，卻不見了，英語都可以說 gone。

瞧，多簡單，我們就來看 go 可以用在多少地方，trust me，相信我，你若學會用 go，英語就很溜了！

>>>

go 表示「變得、成為」的意思，是連綴動詞的用法，go 的後面要接形容詞，例如：go mad、go wild、go bad、go sour、go crazy。go 也可以表示「在某一種狀態中」，例如：go hungry

» The company **went** bankrupt last year.

這家公司去年宣告破產。

* bankrupt ['bæŋkrʌpt]，當形容詞是「破產的」的意思。

» The milk **went** sour.

牛奶變酸了。

* 牛奶壞了，可以用 sour [saʊr]「酸的」這個字，也可以說 go bad。

» Look at the mold on this cheese. It **went** bad.

你看乳酪上的霉。這個乳酪已經壞了。

» I think you're **going** crazy.

我認為你是瘋了。

» After the summer vacation, the children **went** wild.

過了暑假，孩子們都玩野了。

» Our plans failed. I don't know what went wrong.
我們的計畫失敗。我不知道出了什麼差錯。

» The value of the dollar is going down.
美元在貶值。

go 表示消失；時間過去；衰退

» Has your headache gone yet?
你頭痛好了嗎？
＊ go 在這裡是「痛楚消失了」的意思。

» The TV remote control is gone.
電視遙控器不見了。
＊ go 在這裡是「東西不見了」的意思。

» My sight is starting to go.
我的視力開始變差。

» My hearing is going.
我的聽力漸漸衰退。
＊ go 在這裡的意思是表示「衰退、變差」。

>>>

» His parents are all gone. He is on his own.

他的雙親都已過世。他要靠他自己。

＊ 人死了，如果你不願意直接說 die，也可以說 go。

» The summer is going fast.

今年夏天過的真快。

» Time goes quickly when you're busy.

當你忙碌的時候，時間過得很快。

＊ go 用來表示「時間過去了」，後面常接副詞，例如：go fast、go quickly「時間過的真快」、go slowly 表示「時間過的真慢」。

» Where did all the money I gave you go?

我給你的錢都到哪裡去了？

» Two hundred dollars doesn't go far these days.

這年頭，兩百元買不到什麼東西。

＊ go 也可以表示「花錢」或「錢花光了」。

» The piano went for $500.

鋼琴以五百元賣掉。

＊ go 可以當「被賣掉」的意思。

» The bulb in the kitchen is gone.

廚房的燈泡壞了。

＊ go 也可以當「漸漸變弱、壞掉」的意思。

go 表示「從一個地方到另一個地方」

» It's late. I must be going.

天晚了，我該走了。

» The teacher hasn't gone yet.

老師還沒有離開。

» I wanted to go, but Mary wanted to stay.

我想要去，但是瑪莉想要留下來。

» I'll just go and get my coat.

我就去拿我的大衣。

» Shall we go get something to eat?

我們去吃點東西好嗎？

＊ go 後面馬上接另一個動詞的說法，是口語的說法。

» John has gone to New York.

約翰已經到紐約去了。

>>>

» Where are you going?
你要去哪裡？

» We're going to my parents' house for New Year.
我們要去我父母家過新年。

» What time are you going to the airport?
你什麼時候要去機場？

» They all went away and left me alone.
他們都走了，留下我一個人。

» Can we go home?
我們回家好嗎？

» John is too young to go to school.
約翰還太小，不能去上學。

» Make sure this letter goes tonight.
這封信今晚一定要寄。

» There goes the bus.
公車走了。

go可以與must、have to和can連用，用法是「某樣東西或某人must go、have to go或can go」，表示「你必須把該樣東西或某人弄走、丟掉、辭掉或放棄」或「你可以把該樣東西或某人弄走、丟掉、辭掉或放棄」

» That secretary will have to go; she can't even type.

你一定要把那個秘書辭掉，她甚至於連打字都不會。

» The car must go.

這部車子一定要賣掉。

» The TV can go.

這部電視可以拿走。

機器運轉

» The clock isn't going.

這個鐘壞了。

＊如果某個機器goes，也就是說這個機器works，表示「這個機器運作正常」，也就是說「這個機器沒有壞」。

» The engine is still going. Shut it down.

引擎還在轉動。把它關掉。

＊go在這裡是「機器在運轉」的意思。

» Our car won't go.

我們的車子不動。

事情進行的如何

» Is everything going okay?

一切都順利嗎？

» How's it going?

一切都好嗎？

＊ 你如果遇到熟識的人，可以用這句話來問候對方。

» How are things going?

一切都好嗎？

» How did the meeting go?

會議開得如何？

» The meeting went well today.

今天會議開得很順利。

» The game didn't go well for our team.

我們隊球賽打得不好。

» How are things going at work?
上班上得好嗎？

» Business is going well.
生意做得很順利。

放置；可通過；裝得進；塞得進

» The book shelf can go next to the desk.
書架可以放在書桌旁。

» Where can the piano go?
鋼琴要放在哪裡？

» The brooms go in that closet.
掃帚要放在那個櫥櫃裡。
* go 在以上三句話裡是當「放置」的意思。

» Empty cans go in this box for recycling.
空的罐子要放在這個盒子裡，以便回收。

» All these clothes won't go into one suitcase.
這些衣服一個皮箱裝不下。

» Will the desk go through the door?

這張桌子可以過這扇門嗎？

＊ go 在這裡當「可通過、裝得進、塞得進」的意思。

相配；相稱；和諧

» Do green shirt and blue pants go together?

綠色的襯衫和藍色的褲子配起來好看嗎？

＊ 如果兩個顏色 go together，表示「這兩個顏色搭配起來很好看」。

» That green tie and blue shirt don't go together.

那條綠色的領帶和藍色的襯衫不相配。

» Does this tie go well with my shirt?

這條領帶配我的襯衫好看嗎？

＊ 如果某件東西 go with 另一樣東西，表示「這兩樣東西配起來很好看」。

伸展；通向

» This highway goes to New York.

這條高速公路通到紐約。

» The Mississippi river goes from Minnesota to Louisiana.

密西西比河從明尼蘇達州延伸到路易斯安那州。

（音樂等）有某種調子；發某種聲音

» The tune goes something like this.

調子是這樣的。

＊ go 在這裡是「以某一特殊的方式陳述故事，或唱一首歌」的意思。

» A cow goes "moo, moo".

牛的叫聲是「哞、哞」。

go 引伸的意思

» This time he's gone too far.

這一次他是做得太過份了。

＊ go too far 照字面翻譯就是，走得太遠了，也就是說「做得太過份了」。

» What the boss says goes.

老闆說怎樣就怎樣。

» I have five days to go before I take a vacation.

我還有五天就要去休假。

» I've sent out ten applications. There are five more to go.

我已經寄出十封申請表。還有五封要寄。

» For here or to go?

在店裡吃還是外賣？

* 你到餐廳買食物，服務員會問你要「在店裡吃還是要外賣」，英語就是這句話。

» We got some fried chicken to go and ate it at the park.

我們買了一些炸雞，帶到公園去吃。

* 買食物 to go 就是「外賣」，也就是「不在餐廳裡吃，買了食物帶走」的意思。

到某個地方去做某件事情

» Let's go for a walk after lunch.

吃過午飯我們去散步。

» Let's go for a swim this afternoon.

今天下午我們去游泳。

» I am going to go for a jog before breakfast.

早餐之前我想去慢跑一下。

＊ 以上幾句話都是「go for＋你到某個地方之後，要做的事」。

» John has gone skiing in Aspen.

約翰已經到艾斯本滑雪去了。

» Would you like to go shopping today?

你今天要去購物嗎？

＊「go＋動名詞」，表示去做某件事，例如：go swimming「去游泳」，go fishing「去釣魚」，go jogging「去慢跑」，go skiing「去滑雪」。

» Do you want to go to the movies?

你要去看電影嗎？

go 的其它用法

» What do you go by?

怎麼稱呼你？

» I go by Bob.

我叫我鮑伯。

＊ go by 這個片語的意思就是「別人怎麼叫你」或「你喜歡別人怎樣叫你」。

» First place went to Mary.

瑪莉得到第一名。

＊ go 在這裡表示「被給」的意思。

» Five into two won't go.

五除以二，除不盡。

＊ 如果一個數字 into 另一個數字 go，表示「第一個數字除以第二個數字，可以除得盡」。

慣用語特好用

go on sale

- I always like to wait for stuff to go on sale.

我總是喜歡等東西在打折時去買。

go by bus

- We went by plane.

我們搭飛機前往。

- I'll go by bus.

  我要坐公車去前往。

- Are you going by train?

  你要搭火車去的嗎？

  ＊搭乘某樣交通工具去某個地方，英語的成語就是用「go by＋搭乘的交通工具」，例如：go by plane，go by bus，go by train。

口語特常說

There you go.

如果你兒子考試考得不好，他跟你說，我知道我不夠認真，我一定會好好用功，你就可以跟他說 There you go.，這句話在這裡的意思就是「這樣才對嘛！」

如果你的朋友去求職，結果沒被錄用，你也可以跟他說 There you go. 希望下一次會有好消息。There you go. 這句話在這裡的意思是「事情就是這樣」。

Here you go.

如果你開車送朋友回家，到了她家門口，你就可以跟她說 Here you go. 這句話在這裡的意思是「你家到了。」

另外，如果對方要你拿東西給她，你拿了，要遞給她，也可以跟她説 Here you go. 這句話的意思就是「你要的東西在這裡」。

如果你的同事的電腦有問題，你過去幫他弄好，這時候你也可以跟他説 Here you go. All set. 這句話的意思就是「都弄好了」。

There goes...

這句話的意思是表示，因為某件事使得你想要做的事情沒辦法作，或是你要的東西得不到，而你覺得很失望，There goes 後面接的就是「你要的東西」或「你想要做的事情」。例如：你本來想要去歐洲，卻因為原本的計畫取消，使得你沒辦法去，你就可以説 There goes my chance to Europe.「我到歐洲的機會飛了」。

Here she goes again.

如果有一個人常喜歡做一件你不喜歡的事，當她又要做時，你可以説 Here she goes again. 或 There she goes again.

2 come

文法特強調

相對於 go、come 這個字也很有動感。come 也表示從一點到另一點中間的過程，但 come 有一個方向感，是從遠方的一點，朝向你說話者這邊的方向。所以 come 可以表示「來」，可以表示「到達」，更可以表示「有結果了」，因為「有結果」就是「結果出來了」嘛！所以「夢想成真」的英語就叫 a dream come true.

come 還有很多好用、很生動的意思，你看 Oh good, now he comes to. 是什麼意思? 有一個電視廣告，一個年輕的男士接到一位漂亮小姐的電話說，「我的好朋友這個月不會來了，下個月也不會來了。」這位做事不敢當的可憐男士，接到這樣的通知，當場昏倒，假如，你正好在旁邊，趕忙扶著他，搖搖他，直到他「嚶」一聲，張開眼睛，你就説，Oh good, now he comes to.，知道意思了吧，他「甦醒」了，因為他被嚇走的三魂七魄又 come to 了！

來

» Come here.
過來。

» Would you like to come to our party?
你要不要來參加我們的宴會？

» Would you like to come to the dance with me?
你要不要跟我去參加舞會？

» Can Mary come too?
瑪莉也可以來嗎？

» Mary is coming later on.
瑪莉等一下會來。

» Are you coming back Friday?

你星期五要回來嗎？

» Can I come and see you tomorrow?
我明天可以來看你嗎？

» What day are your friends coming to dinner?
你的朋友哪一天要來吃晚餐？

» Someone is coming to fix the TV.
有人會來修理電視。

» Did you come by plane or by train?
你搭飛機還是乘火車來？

到達

» The bill has come at a bad time.
帳單來的不是時候。

» When does the train come?
火車什麼時候到？

» Labor and management finally came to an

agreement.
勞資雙方終於達成協議。

» The problem has come to my attention.
我已經注意到這個問題。

位於

» Eight comes before nine.
八在九的前面。

» Nine comes after eight.
九在八的後面。

總共

» Your grocery bill comes to $50.00
你買的雜貨總共是五十元。

達到

» The jacket comes down to the knees.
這件夾克長到膝蓋。

被出售；被生產

» Does this dress come in other colors?
這件洋裝你們有別的顏色嗎？

» Do those shoes come in my size?
那雙鞋子有我的尺寸嗎？

» These shoes come in four sizes.
這雙鞋子有四種尺寸。

變成；成為

» Mary, your shoelaces have come untied.
瑪莉，你的鞋帶沒繫好。

» A button on my shirt came loose and fell off.
我的襯衫有一顆扣子鬆了，結果掉了。

» The bottle came open in my bag.
瓶蓋在我的袋子裡鬆開。

排重要性；名次

» My family always comes before anything.
我的家庭是最重要的。

» For John, his career always comes first.
對約翰來說，事業最重要。

» At the tournament, we came last.
我們比賽得到最後一名。

來自

» Mary comes from a large family.
瑪莉來自一個大家庭。

» Where do you come from?
你從哪裡來的？

慣用語特好用

come along

- Do you mind if I come along with you?

你介意我跟你一起去嗎？

＊come along 是「跟著某人到某個地方去」的意思。

come over

- Why don't you come over Friday?

  你何不星期五過來我家？

  ＊come over 是「來拜訪某人」的意思。

come for

- I have come for Mary. Is she ready?

  我來接瑪莉。她準備好了嗎？

- When is John coming for you?

  約翰什麼時候要來接你？

  ＊come for 某人，表示「來接某人去某個地方」。

口語特常說

Come on.

Come on. 這句話有好幾個意思，從 Come on. 後面所接的句子，可以知道 Come on. 表示什麼意思。

Come on 的第一個意思是表示「鼓勵」，例如：Come on, you can do it.「來吧，你做得到的」。

Come on 的第二個意思是表示「懷疑」，例如：Oh come on, you can't fool me.「得了，我不會被騙的」。

Come on 的第三個意思是表示「不耐煩」，例如：Come on, we're going to miss the plane.「快點，我們會趕不上飛機」。

Come off it.

Come off it. 這句話是「夠了」的意思，表示你的不悅，例如：Oh, come off it! Stop talking that nonsense!「夠了，不要再胡說」。

How come

How come 是一句口語，是「為什麼」的意思。

3

make

文法特強調

make 這個字，學校裡多半教你「作」或「製造」的意思，這只對了一半。make 當然是「製造」的意思，但是 make 所強調的，不是製造，而是強調製造「成功」！也就是說，如果沒有從「製造的過程」達到「成功的結果」，make 就沒有意義，所以英語裏有一句話說 make or break。break 是「斷掉」的意思，剛好與 make 押韻，make or break 的意思是：「不成功便成仁」，也就是「成敗在此一舉！」

像前美國總統 Clinton 在白宮與 L 小姐做了一些休閒小運動，檢察官一定要把兩人之間的「公共關係」解釋成「公眾關係」，硬是在一個星期五把兩人當時所做的事、所說的話，記錄下來，送到美國國會，準備讓它原音重現，向全世界發表，要 Clinton 幹不成總統。那個週末那兩天，白宮可忙壞了，忙著到處消音闢謠，讓損傷減到最低，對 Clinton 來説，那個週末就是他 make or break 的生死關頭！

make 有這種「做成」的含意，所以賺錢叫 make money，可不是真的去「印製」錢！交朋友是 make friends。考試上榜、找到工作、被女士拒絕五百回約會，終於答應與你一起去散步一分鐘，你都可以説 I made it.，「我成功了！」，這裡的 I made it. 可不是：「那是我做的」噢！

製作

» Would you make a cake for Mary's birthday?

你可不可以做個蛋糕給瑪莉過生日？

» My mom made the dress for me.

我的母親做這件洋裝給我。

» The car was made in Japan.

這部車子是日本製的。

» We are making a documentary about World War II.
我們在製作有關第二次世界大戰的記錄影片。

» Shall I make you a cup of coffee?
你要我泡杯咖啡給你嗎？

做…

» He made a quick decision to buy the car.
他很快的做了決定要買這部車。

» May I make a suggestion?
我可以提個建議嗎？

make 後面接「一些有關說話」的字，表示某人說了甚麼話。

» I'd like to make an appointment with Mr. Lin.
我要跟林先生約個時間見面。
＊ 這句話通常用在你要跟林先生的秘書約時間。

使得某人或某樣東西…

» Spoiled milk will make you sick.
壞了的牛奶會使你生病。

make 當使役動詞，使；促使；迫使

» What makes you say that?
你為什麼那樣說？

» We can't make the rock move.
我們推不動石頭。

» Her mother made her do her homework.
她的母親強迫她做功課。

賺錢

» How much do you think she makes?
你認為她賺多少錢？

» I guess she makes about $35,000 a year.
我猜她的年薪是三萬五左右。

» I made $5000 out of selling my car.
我賣掉我的車子賺了五千元。

» She makes good money as a pianist.
她當鋼琴家賺很多錢。

» Our company made a big profit this year.
今年我們公司賺很多錢。

» Mary makes her living by writing books.
瑪莉靠寫作為生。

等於

» Two and three make five.
二加三等於五。

» Two times three makes six.
二乘以三等於六。

» Twelve inches make a foot.
十二吋是一尺。

>>>

因有某種特點、品質足以成功

» I don't think she'll make a good doctor.

我不認為她會是一個好醫生。

» The book will make a good movie.

這本書可以拍出一部好電影。

趕上；及時到達

» They didn't make the 10 o'clock flight.

他們沒趕上十點的班機。

» Do we have time to make the seven o'clock showing of the movie?

我們有時間趕上七點那一場電影嗎？

＊ make 在以上兩句話裡是「趕到某個特定地方」的意思。

» Do you think we can make the town before nightfall?

你認為我們天黑之前可以到鎮上嗎？

» Will you be able to make the Friday

meeting?

星期五的會議你能來參加嗎？

» I'm sorry, I can't make Tuesday after all.

很抱歉，我星期二終究不能來。

* make 在這裡的意思是「能夠去一個已經訂好時間的場合」，它的用法有：make the meeting, make the party, make Friday 等等。

進入校隊

» John hopes to make the football team this year.

約翰希望他今年能夠進足球隊。

» Did your sister make the math team?

你妹妹有沒有進數學校隊？

* 進學校的校隊，如：球賽的校隊或學科競賽的校隊，英語就是 make the team。

其它用法

» The scandal made the headlines.

這件醜聞成了頭條新聞。

慣用語特好用

make friends with

» I tried to make friends with Mary, but she didn't seem to like me.

我想跟瑪莉作朋友，但是她好像不喜歡我。

* make friends with 就是「跟某人作朋友」的意思。

make the bed

» I make my bed every morning.

我每天早上都整理床鋪。

* make the bed 就是「鋪床、整理床鋪」的意思。

make believe

» We made believe we were prince and princess.

我們假裝我們是王子和公主。

* make believe 是「假裝」的意思。

make something up

» Can I **make up** the test I missed?

我可以補考嗎？

＊make something up 是「補償」或「重做」的意思。

» What she said was not true. She **made** it **up**.

她所說的並不是真的。她杜撰的。

＊make something up 也可以是「杜撰」的意思。

口語特常說

make it

make it 這句口語，基本上的意思是「做得到」的意思，例如：你們快趕不上火車了，所以你說，如果我們用跑的話，應該趕得上，這裡的「趕得上」英語就是 make it，整句話的說法就是，If we run, we should make it.。

如果說，某人在某一行業很成功，也可以說某人 make it，例如：有人說她想成為明星，你說，我認為你做不到，英語就是 I don't think you can make it.

make it 也可以用在「可以參加某個活動或會議」，例如：星期六朋友家有個宴會，你不能去參加，你跟他說抱歉，不能來參加，英語就是 I'm sorry, but I won't be able to make it to the party on Saturday.

that makes two of us

That makes two of us. 這句話是用在，你同意對方說的話，或是你告訴對方說，你所遇到的事，我也遇到了。

make yourself at home

Make yourself at home. 這句話是用在，當有人來你家作客時，你要他別拘束，放輕鬆，讓你自己好像在你自己家裡一樣。

4 take

文法特強調

take 和 make 這兩個字，不但發音很接近，寫起來很類似，在意思上，也有稍微共通的地方。make 是「製造、做」，take 也有「做」的意思。但是 take 不強調一般性的「做」或做「成功」，而是強調做事的「麻煩」、要下功夫才能做。

所以當你最初在學校裡學 take 這個字，老師說是「拿」的意思。拿到東西本來就是對自己有利的事，但天下沒有白吃的午餐，所以要「拿」就必須要下功夫，所以「下功夫去做」，就是 take 最原始的含意。

明白了這個含意，你就知道為什麼「花費」時間，也是用 take，例如 It takes two weeks to do.「那得花上兩星期去做」，還有，Take time. 是「別急，慢慢來」，說穿了，就是叫別人不用趕，可以多「花一點時間」，沒關係！另外，It takes two men to do.是「那要兩個大男人才做得來。」，一聽就知道不輕鬆，肯定是耗力氣的事。

說英語，就是要會用這種有含意、生動的字來表達，不然學了再多的英語單字，別人聽了半天，還是聽攏嘸，不知道您的意下如何？

當然，從「拿」的含意，又可延伸出很多生動的意義來，例如，買東西說 I'll take it. 意思是：我就「買」這個！，又如，Do you take credit cards?「你們收信用卡嗎？」，只要你想用英語說話，不會說 take 這個字，保證你三分鐘不到，就結結巴巴，說不下去了！

take 可以用在，你要對方把某樣東西或某人帶著，拿到他要去的地方

» **Take** an umbrella with you. It looks like it will rain.

帶把傘，看起來會下雨。

» When you go to the movies, can you **take** Mary with you?

如果你要去看電影，可不可以帶瑪莉一起去？

» Why don't you take Mary to a movie?
你為什麼不帶瑪莉去看電影？

take 也可以用在，帶某人去某個地方，或把某樣東西拿到某個地方去。

» I'll take Mary with me when I go to the fair.
我要去市集的時候，會帶瑪莉一起去。

» Can you take me to the store?
你可以帶我去商店嗎？

» John took our car to the garage to be repaired.
約翰把我們的車子開去修車廠修理。

» May I take your bags to your room?
你要我把你的行李拿到你的房間嗎？
＊ 這是旅館服務員對到旅館投宿的客人說的話。

take 後面跟一些不同的名詞，表示你所做的

» We take a vacation every May.
我們每年五月都去度假。

» I'm going to take a walk. Do you want to come along?

我要去散步。你要不要一起來？

» It's time for you to take a bath.

你該去洗澡了。

» We would like to take a 10-day trip.

我們要去旅行十天。

需要

» It took us two hours to get there.

我們花了兩小時才能到那裡。

» How long will it take to type the letter?

打這封信要多久？

» The car only takes unleaded.

這部車子只能加無鉛汽油。

» John's got what it takes to be a great actor.

約翰有成為好演員的特質。

» How many stamps will this letter take?
這封信需要幾張郵票？

» How long does first class mail take?
第一類郵件要多久才會到？

修課，參加考試

» I am planning to take English with Ms. Lin.
我計畫上林老師的英文課。

» I am taking two science classes this semester.
這學期我上了兩門科學課。

» I only had to take 6 credit hours my senior year.
我大四只需修六學分的課。

吃的意思

» Do you want to take an aspirin for your headache?
你頭痛要不要吃一顆阿斯匹靈？

» He took some tea with his lunch.

他吃午餐時也喝茶。

» Do you want to take lunch together?

你要不要一起去吃午餐？

» John was caught taking drugs.

約翰被抓到吸食毒品。

＊ take drugs 是「吸食毒品」的意思，不是一般生病時吃藥。

接受

» If I were you, I'd take the job.

如果我是你，我會接受這個工作。

» I'll take it.

好，我要了。

＊ 這句話是用在購物或商務談判，你決定要買或接受條件時的說法。

» Do you take credit cards?

你們收信用卡嗎？

» Do you take traveler's checks?

你們收旅行支票嗎？

» The car won't take any more people.

這部車沒辦法再容納任何一個人。

＊ take 在這裡是「有空位容納」的意思。

» How did she take it when she got fired?

她被開除的時候，還能承受嗎？

take 的其它用法

» May I take your order?

你要點菜了嗎？

＊ 在餐廳服務生問客人的話。

» Please take some cake and drinks.

請拿些蛋糕和飲料。

＊ 在宴會中，主人要你拿些東西吃。

» I took several pictures of the cabin we stayed in.

我照了幾張我們住的木屋的相片。

» He took my temperature and blood pressure.
他量我的體溫和血壓。

» I take it you've heard that John was fired.
我假設你已經知道約翰被開除了。

» Which bus do you want to take?
你要搭哪一班公車？

» John took all the credit.
約翰搶去所有的功勞。

» I can't take any more of his lies.
我已經受不了他的謊話連篇。

慣用語特好用

take sides

- He always takes sides with Mary.
他總是偏袒瑪莉。
* take sides 就是「偏袒」的意思，偏袒某人或偏袒某一

邊，英語就是 take sides with 某人或某一邊。

take care of

- Will you take care of my plants while I'm away?

  我不在的時候，你可以照料我的花草嗎？

  * take care of 就是「照顧、照料」的意思。

take someone in

- Don't let her innocent smile take you in.

  別讓她天真無邪的笑容把你騙了。

  * take 某人 in，就是「欺騙某人」的意思。

take me wrong

- Don't take me wrong.

  別誤會我的意思。

口語特常說

Could I take a message?

Could I take a message? 這句話是用在，有人

打電話來要找的人正好不在，你問對方要不要留個話，給他要找的人。

Take it easy.

Take it easy. 這句話，可以用作「告別語」，請對方保重。

Take it easy. 也表示「休息」、「放鬆」的意思，這句話大多用在工作的很辛苦，或是身體有不適時，例如：你說你這個週末需要休息一下，英語的說法就是 I'm going to take it easy this weekend.，或是你叫對方多休息，英語的說法就是 You'd better take it easy.

文法特強調

bring 這個字頂有意思的。一般學英語，總是把它拿來與 take 一起學，這是因為 take 是「拿去」，而 bring 是「拿來」，英文老師總喜歡把這兩個字的區別著重在「去」和「來」上面，例如：Take an umbrella with you是「帶把雨傘去吧！」，而 Bring an umbrella with you. 是「帶把傘來唷」。

不過，想一想，什麼是「去」？什麼是「來」？這是位置的問題。「去」是「離開」説話者，「來」則是「朝向」説話者。

所以 Bring an umbrella with you. 已經表示説話的人在叮嚀對方，來的時候要帶傘。而 Take an umbrella with you. 是指對方要離開了，説話者叮嚀對方走的時候要帶傘。

去和來的觀念，有時候很容易弄混，不要這

樣區別。講英語時，談到「去」，假如是「去」向說話者所在的地方，或是「去」說話者將會去的地方，雖然是「去」，卻要用 bring，例如：你要去參加 party 宴會，要帶女朋友一起「去」的話，因為女朋友是與你一道去，這時，你對宴會的主人說，I will bring my girlfriend.「我會帶著女朋友去（來）參加」，因為你是說話者，你也會去宴會。

而假如你要請一個人帶你去一個地方，他說 Okay, I will take you there.「好，我帶你去」，他是說話的人，他必須離開他說話當時的所在，才能帶你去你要去的地方，所以他說 take you there.

bring 還有其他的意思，雖然含意也是「帶來」的意思，但運用起來卻非常美妙，例如，中國人歡迎朋友，經常說「是什麼風把你吹來呀？」，英語就是用 bring 這個字，底下會有說明，請仔細閱讀。

bring 是用在，你要對方帶著某件東西或某個人到你這裡來，或帶到你會去的地方，也可以是你自己帶著去某個地方。

» I left my book at your house. Could you

bring it to school tomorrow?

我的書留在你家。你明天可以帶去學校嗎？

＊ 請對方把某樣東西帶到你會去的地方。

» Would you bring me some napkins?

請你拿一些紙巾給我？

＊ 請對方把某樣東西帶到你這裡來。

» Did you bring any books to read?

你有沒有帶書來讀？

» Mary brought a friend to the party.

瑪莉帶一個朋友去參加宴會。

＊ 說某人帶另一個人到某個地方，而你也在場。

» I bring an umbrella with me in case it rains.

我帶著一把傘，萬一下雨用得到。

＊ 你說你自己帶著某樣東西。

bring 也用在，表示帶東西去「給」某人。另外，你告訴對方說，你會把某樣東西帶去給他，不管他人在何處，也用 bring。

» Hold on, I'll bring you a towel.

別動，我拿條毛巾給你。

＊告訴對方，你會拿東西給他。

» They **brought** her everything she asked.

他們帶給她，她所要求的一切東西。

＊bring 在這裡是，帶東西去「給」某人。

當有人邀你去參加宴會，你問對方需要你帶東西去嗎，以下是一些很漂亮的說法，這種英語要多記多說，表示你很「上道」。

» Is there anything I could **bring**?

需要我帶什麼東西來嗎？

» What shall I **bring**?

我該帶什麼來？

» Can I **bring** the drinks?

我帶飲料來好嗎？

引起

» The heavy rain will **bring** floods.

這場豪雨會帶來水災。

Take 和 bring 的區別

» Take an umbrella with you in case it rains.
帶把傘去，以防萬一下雨。

» I bring an umbrella with me in case it rains.
我帶著一把傘，以防萬一下雨。

＊ 上句的 take 顯示出對方要離開，你叮嚀著他把雨傘帶著。下句的 bring 是你說你自己隨身帶著某樣東西。

» When you're in Taipei, I'll take you to the zoo.
當你來台北的時候，我會帶你去動物園。

» When I'm in Taipei, bring your boyfriend to see me.
我來台北的時候，帶你的男朋友來看我。

＊ 上句的 take 是表示你說話時，不在動物園。下句的 bring 是說，你叫對方帶某人到你這裡來。

口語特常說

Just bring yourself.

如果有人邀你去參加她舉辦的宴會，你問她，你需要帶什麼東西來嗎，對方如果不需要你帶什麼東西過去，她可以說 Just bring yourself.，意思就是說「妳人來就好了，不要帶什麼東西來」。

What brings you here?

中文說的「什麼風把你吹來了？」，英語的說法就是 What brings you here?

文法特強調

學習英文的時候，把 give 和 take 一起學是很有深意的。give 的原意是「給」，而 take 是「拿」，這兩個字放在一起，give and take 就是「不要光是拿，也得給」，換句話說，就是勸人要「佔點便宜、吃點虧」。

既然 give 的含意不限在指有形的「遞給」，也包括了無形的給予，所以它可以表達的意義空間就大了，舉凡 give two weeks「給」時間，give you trouble「給」人家帶來不方便，give me a headache「給」別人搞得頭疼、不舒服等等，都可以用 give。

給；供給；提供

» Can you give me a ride to school?

你可以載我去學校嗎？

＊ give 在這裡是「提供」的意思。

» The doctor gave him something for the pain.

醫生給他一些止痛的藥。

» What did John give you for your birthday?

約翰給你什麼生日禮物？

» Give the rabbit some carrots.

給那隻兔子一些紅蘿蔔。

» Cows give milk.

母牛製造牛奶。

＊ give 在這裡是「製造」的意思。

» Can you give me a hand?

你可以幫我一個忙嗎？

＊ give 在這裡是「給予幫忙」的意思。

» I'll give you a call tonight.

我今晚會打個電話給你。

» We are giving Mary a wedding shower Sunday afternoon.

星期天下午我們要為瑪莉舉辦一個結婚送禮會。

* give 在這裡是「舉辦宴會」的意思。

» My English teacher gave us a lot of homework today.

今天我的英文老師給我們許多功課。

» My boss is always giving me a hard time these days.

我老闆最近老是找我的麻煩。

» This new computer system is giving us a lot of trouble.

這個新的電腦系統給我們很多麻煩。

提供消息；資訊

» The first chapter gives a broad outline of the book.

第一篇大概說明了這本書的大綱。

» Can you give me some information on buying a new car?

你能不能在買新車方面給我一些意見？

» I gave Mary my word that I'd take her to the movies.

我已經答應瑪莉，我要帶她去看電影。

＊ give 某人 my word，就是「我答應某人」的意思。

容許

» You should give yourself an hour to drive to the airport.

你要開到機場，需要給你自己一小時的時間。

» I'll give you another chance to make up.

我再給你一次機會補救。

時間

» Give him time. It's always hard to learn another language.

給他一些時間，學外國語言總是困難的。

» John and Susan are going to get married?I give it two months.

約翰和蘇珊要結婚？我估計這婚姻只能維持兩個月。

✻ 當你說你「give it 多少時間」的時候，就是表示你不認為這件事能持久，你估計頂多能維持到你說的時間。

付

» I'll give you $5,000 for your old car.

你那部舊車我想用五千元來買。

» GE's bond gives a good return of ten percent a year.

GE 公司的債券一年有百分之十的好回收。

give 的其它用法

» The noise gave me a real headache.

那噪音讓我頭很痛。

» Don't come too close. I don't want to give you my cold.

不要太靠近我。我不想傳染感冒給你。

＊ give 在這裡是「傳染疾病給別人」的意思。

» The leather will give a little after you've worn the shoes a while.

這雙鞋子你穿了一段時間之後，皮革就會軟一點。

＊ 如果某種材料 gives，那就是說你若加壓力，它就會彎曲或延伸。

» I tried to move the box, but it wouldn't give an inch.

我想要推動這個盒子，但是完全推不動。

＊ give 在這裡是「因為外力的推動而移動」的意思。

» He was given two years.

他被判處兩年的徒刑。

＊ give 在這裡是「法院的判決」的意思。

慣用語特好用

give up

• The doctor asked him to give up smoking.

醫生要他戒煙。

＊give up something 就是「停止做某件事情」的意思。

Don't give up.

別放棄。

口語特常說

Don't give me that.

當對方遲到，他向你解釋他為什麼遲到的原因，而你知道他只是在編造理由時，你就可以跟他說 Don't give me that.。意思是，你不相信對方說的話，你叫他不要跟你說那些編造的話。

I give it six weeks.

當你說你「give it 多少時間」的時候，就是表示你不認為這件事能持久，你估計頂多能維持到你說的時間。

7 run

文法特強調

拿 run 這個字去問英文的初學者，他一定説，「簡單！就是「跑」的意思嘛」，他説得沒錯，但 run 最生動的含意不是「跑」，而是「運轉」，有種運轉、自強不息的感覺。人「跑」的時候有這種感覺，機器「轉動」的時候有這種感覺，而生意上的「營運」也有這種生生不息的感覺，所以全部都用 run 來表示。

各級組織的競選，所有參加的候選人，也要馬不停蹄地跑，所以競選也是用 run。甚至，水的流動，也可以用 run 呢！你可以感覺出來 run 的動感嗎？

跑

» If we run, we should catch the bus.
如果我們用跑的話，我們應該可以趕上公車。

» Are you going to run the marathon?
你要參加馬拉松比賽嗎？

» John is running in the 100-meter race.
約翰在跑一百公尺賽跑。

» Run and tell Mary "CSI" is on.
你趕快去告訴瑪莉「CIS 犯罪現場」開演了。

經營

» I would like to run my own cafe one day.
有一天我想自己開一間小館子。

» Could you run the store for me while I'm gone?
我不在的時候，你可以幫我看店嗎？

競選

» I am going to run against John for PTA president.

我要跟約翰競選家長會會長。

» Did you hear who is running against Clinton?

你有沒有聽說誰要跟克林頓競選？

» Do you know who is running for president?

你知道誰要競選總統嗎？

» Who is planning to run for mayor?

誰計畫要競選市長？

操作；機器的運轉

» Is your new car running okay?

你的車子跑得還好嗎？

» The new system won't be up and running until next month.

新系統要在下個月才能裝好，開始運轉。

» Do you know how to run a tractor?
你知道如何操作拖曳機嗎？

車子在跑動

» The buses don't run on Sundays.
公車星期天不開。

» The bus runs past my house every hour.
公車每一個小時經過我家一次。

水或液體的流動

» Don't leave the faucet running.
別讓水龍頭流個不停。

» Could you run me a hot bath?
幫我準備熱水洗澡好嗎？
* run a bath 的意思就是「把浴缸放滿水」。

其他用法

» The color ran when my mom washed my red shirt.

我媽洗我的紅色襯衫時，顏色染到其他的衣服。

＊ 如果你洗衣服時，其中一件紅色的衣服染到其他的衣服，那英語就是 The color ran.。

» Look, the ink on the letter ran.

你看，這封信上的墨水糊掉了。

＊ 如果紙張弄濕了，紙上的墨水也會糊掉，它的英語就是，The ink on the letter ran.。

» Mary is running a temperature of a 40-degree.

瑪莉發燒到四十度。

» The meeting is running late. It won't be over until 11:00.

會議超過預定的時間。十一點才會結束。

» He ran first in the 100-meter race.

他在一百米賽跑中得第一名。

» It's late. I've got to run now.

已經很晚了。我該走了。

＊ run 在這裡的意思是「要離開某個地方」。

» Her pantyhose ran and made a big hole.

她的褲襪破了一個大洞。

＊ 襪子、褲襪 run，就是「襪子、褲襪破了」。

» We ran an ad to hire an editor.

我們登廣告要請一位編輯。

慣用語特好用

run an errand

- I've got to run an errand. I'll be back in a minute.

  我有事情要去做。一會兒就回來。

  ＊ run an errand 就是「去做一件事情」的意思。

run out of

- I ran out of milk while I was baking the cakes.

  我在做蛋糕的時候，牛奶都用完了。

  ＊ run out of 某樣東西，就是「把某樣東西通通用完」的意思。

>>>

run low on

- We are low on eggs.

我們的蛋剩下不多。

＊ run low on 某樣東西，就是「某樣東西不夠」或「某樣東西剩下不多」的意思。

口語特常說

It runs in the family.

當我們說到某人很聰明，事實上他家裡每一個人都很聰明，英語的說法就是 It runs in the family. 意思是說「他的聰明是家傳的」。又如：某人的頭髮是紅色的，而你知道她家每個人的頭髮都是紅色的，英語的說法也是這句話 It runs in the family.

8 say

文法特強調

say 這個字很妙，它表面上的意義是「說」，不過，你可不要誤解，把「說」侷限在「講話」或「開口說話」，在很多情況下，「說」是不用開口的，你若是一位小姐，我對你說：「小姐，你的眼睛會說話！」你肯定窩心得不得了，但你的眼睛開口了嗎？所以說，say 的概念包括資訊的提供，傳達有聲與無聲的訊息，情境的涵蓋面比「說話」的概念寬廣太多了。

理解這種含意，你馬上就可知道下列這些生動的英語了：What does your watch say?「你的錶現在幾點？」、I say Mary can't be a girl.「我說呀，瑪莉根本不可能是個女的！」，你看，這就是 say 的妙用，在這裡充分表現了我的自信與蠻橫，不管如何，我就是一口咬定瑪莉不像個女性！

>>>

說話

» What did Mary say?
瑪莉說什麼？

» Mary said she would do the dishes.
瑪莉說她會洗碗。

» She didn't say when she will be back.
她沒有說她什麼時候會回來。

» I don't believe anything he says.
我不相信他所說的。

» Does anyone else have anything to say?
有誰還要說什麼嗎？

» I'd just like to say a few words about the plan.
關於這個計畫，我只想要簡短的說明一下。
* say a few words 的意思就是「簡短的說明一下」的意思。

» The law says anyone under 18 can't buy cigarettes.
法律規定，任何人十八歲以下不可以買香菸。

» Remember to say good-bye when you're leaving.
你要離開的時候，要說再見。

» Did you say thanks to the driver when you got off the bus?
你下車的時候有沒有跟司機說謝謝？

用寫的消息或數字

» My watch says it's 5:30.
我手錶的時間是五點三十分。

» What did Mary say in her letter?
瑪莉的信上說什麼？

» It said in the paper that 200 people were killed.
報上說有兩百個人被殺。

意思是

» What do you think the writer is saying in this book?
你認為作者這本書要說什麼？

» Are you saying I'm not qualified?
你的意思是說我不夠資格？

» So what you are saying is, you don't want to join us.
那你的意思是說，你不想加入我們。

» The picture doesn't say much to me.
這張圖畫我看不懂。
＊ say 在這裡的意思是「有意義，所以別人能夠瞭解」。

建議；假設

» I say we should give him a piece of our mind.
我建議我們應該好好的說他一頓。
＊ give 某人 a piece of 某人的 mind，意思就是「責罵某人」。

» Let's say you fail the test, then what?
假設你考不及格，那又怎麼樣？

» Just say you won the lottery. What would you do?
假設你贏得彩券。你要做什麼？

＊ 以上兩句話裡，say 的意思就是「假設某件事會發生」的意思。

慣用語特好用

say something about someone

- I think that Mary must have said something about me to you.
  我知道瑪莉跟你說我怎麼樣。

口語特常說

say yes

如果你要朋友跟你一起去看電影，她還猶疑不決，可能有拒絕的意思，你要求她答應，英語可以說，Oh, please say yes!「噢，拜託你說一聲」「好」。

say so

如果有人問你一件事，例如：對方問你，你認為會下雨嗎，而你認為不會，英語的說法就是，I wouldn't say so.

9 speak

文法特強調

前面説過，say 不一定要開口，那英語有沒有一定得「開口」的「説」這種字呢？答案是：有！就是 speak。speak 通常都是有聲音的，所以擴音器、音箱就稱為 speaker。

say 著重在説出來或所提供的訊息內容，而 speak 是強調「講」的動作或能力，所以罵人的時候，叫對方回答你的問話，對方嚇得聲細如蚊，你吼著他：Speak up!「大聲一點！」，這時，你不會用 say 這個字。還有「我能講英語」是 I can speak English.，表示能力。

跟某人說話

» May I **speak with** Mary?

我想跟瑪莉談話。

＊這句話是用在，你告訴接電話的人或是接待的人，你要找某人談話。

» John would like to speak with you for a moment.

約翰要跟你談一下。

＊speak with 是「跟某人談話，或談事情」的意思。

» I'm angry with him and I refuse to speak to him.

我生他的氣，我拒絕跟他說話。

＊speak to 是「跟某人說話」的意思。

» I was so shocked I couldn't speak.

我嚇得講不出話來。

＊speak 在這裡是「發出聲音說話」的意思。

» Do you speak English?

你會說英語嗎？

＊speak 在這裡是「會講某一種語言」的意思。

» Who is going to speak at the conference?

這次會議誰要來演說？

» The President will speak on the television tonight.

總統將在今晚的電視上演說。

＊ speak在以上兩句話裡，都是「正式發表演說」的意思。

» They had a fight and are not speaking to each other.

他們吵架了，彼此不講話。

» The policeman spoke of the accident.

警察談論這次的車禍。

＊ speak of是「談論某件事情」的意思。

慣用語特好用

generally speaking

» Generally speaking, I'm happy with your work.

總括來說，我滿意你的工作。

speak highly of

» Everyone speaks very highly of Mary.
每個人都說瑪莉很好。

speak up

» I can hardly hear you. Would you speak up?
我幾乎聽不到你說的話。你講大聲一點好嗎？
* speak up，就是「講大聲一點」的意思。

talk

文法特強調

talk也是「說」的意思，但含意著重在有對象、有重點的說話。所以I am talking to you.是「我在對你說話呢！」，這句話已經很明顯的對聽話者的心不在焉，表示極端不滿，這樣講已經夠生動了，對方絕對聽得出你的不滿。

跟某人說話

» Who was that you were **talking** to at the party?
宴會中跟你說話的是誰？

» We were **talking about** the blackout last

night.

我們正在談昨晚停電的事。

» I need to talk with you about my salary.

我要跟你談談我的薪水的問題。

＊ talk with 某人 about 某件事情，它的意思就是「跟某人談某件嚴肅的事情」。

» Most babies start to talk by 18 months.

大多數的嬰孩十八個月時開始說話。

» Can you imagine that computers would be able to talk?

電腦會說話，你能想像得到嗎？

＊ talk 在以上兩句話裡的意思就是「開口說話」。

» Mary and John are not talking.

瑪莉和約翰兩個人彼此不講話。

＊ 如果兩個人 are not talking，表示「他們兩個人吵架，彼此都拒絕跟對方說話」。

» Lovers talk with their eyes.

戀人用眉目傳情。

» Though they tortured him, he refused to **talk**.

雖然他們拷問他，但是他拒絕招供。

＊ talk 在這裡是「招供」的意思。

» Stop **talking** sports. Let's talk business.

不要談體育。我們來談正事吧。

＊ talk 可以用在 talk sports，talk politics，talk business，表示「談論體育、談論政治、談論正事等等」。

慣用語特好用

talk someone out of something

» This is my call, and you can't **talk me out of it**.

決定權是我的，你不可能叫我放棄。

＊ talk someone out of something 就是「勸某人放棄」的意思。

talk back to

» John doesn't like anyone talking back to him.

約翰不喜歡別人回嘴。

＊ talk back to 就是「回嘴」的意思。

口語特常說

People will talk.

有時我們要告誡孩子，有些事情不能做，因為怕別人說閒話，所以我們會說，不要這麼做，「人家會說閒話」或「別人會說長道短」，英語的說法就是 People will talk.

11 tell

文法特強調

tell這個字，若是當成「告訴」某人某事、「跟某人說」，相信很多人是會用的，例如：Tell me the truth.「跟我講實話」。要注意的是tell的過去式是told，一般用過去式的情況很多，例如I told him I was coming.「我跟他講了，我會來」。

不過tell要是沒有明確的對象，不是用在tell you「告訴你」、tell me「告訴我」，tell them「告訴他們」等等，那很可能就是表示「指出來」、「認出來」、「分辨出來」，這樣的用法，很多人可能就不會用了。請注意看下面的説明，好好的感覺一下tell的用法。

告訴

» Could you tell me a bedtime story?

你能不能跟我講一個床邊故事？

» Tell us about your vacation.

跟我們講你去度假的情形。

命令

» Stop trying to tell me what to do all the time.

不要總是告訴我要怎麼做。

» Don't tell me how to behave in public.

不要告訴我在公眾場合要怎麼做。

» The teacher told all the children to stop talking.

老師要所有的小朋友不要再說話。

看出來

» How can you tell he dyed his hair?

你怎麼看得出來他的頭髮染了顏色？

» I could tell she was mad at me.
我看得出來她生我的氣。

» I could tell it was John by the way he walks.
從他走路的樣子，我就看得出來那是約翰。

» I can never tell Jack and John apart.
我沒辦法分得出，誰是傑克、誰是約翰。

» I have trouble telling the difference between a gerund and a participle.
動名詞和分詞的區別，我分不出來。

其它的用法

» I told you she wouldn't help you.
我告訴你了，她不會幫你忙。

» The beeper tells you that you've left the lights on.
嗶嗶聲在告訴你，你沒關燈。

» I'm going to tell your mother on you.

我要去跟你母親說你所做的壞事。

* tell 在這裡的意思是「揭發某人所做的壞事」。

慣用語特好用

tell the time

- John is four years old, and he can tell the time.

  約翰四歲，他會看時間。

  * tell the time 就是「看時鐘或是手錶，知道現在是幾點幾分」的意思。

to tell you the truth

- To tell you the truth, I don't like her.

  跟你說實話，我不喜歡她。

口語特常說

I'll tell you what

I'll tell you what 這句話是用在，大家遇到一些問題需要解決，你要提出解決的方案時，例如：你的室友正好有期終考，忙得連煮飯的時間都沒有，你想幫他在你回家的路上，買個三明治給他吃，英語的說法就是，I'll tell you what, I'll get you a sandwich to eat on my way home.

You're telling me.

You're telling me. 這句話用在當有人說一件事，這件事你已經知道，而且你也同意他的說法時，例如：天氣很熱，約翰走進來，說「這種天氣真令人受不了」，而你也正覺得熱得受不了，你就可以回答說 You're telling me.

文法特強調

相信只要你在學校裡學過英語，你一定學過 ask 這個字，也一定知道 ask 的意思是「問」。但是「問」有很多種含意，在中文是這樣，在英語裡也是這樣，例如你可以因為不知道而問，你也可以問人家要東西，這些都可以用 ask 這個字。這是比較簡單的。

中文一般請別人幫忙，不是用「請」，就是用「求」，以示「人在難中要低頭」，希望動了對方的惻隱之心，但英美國家的人要別人幫忙，一般來講是用問的，例如：Would you help me?、Can you give me a hand?「幫個忙，行嗎？」，所以請求人家幫忙就說是 ask for help。

更妙的是，因為邀請人家做事用 ask 這個字，所以也有了 ask for trouble 這樣的說法，直譯是

「邀請麻煩」，意思就是，「討打呀？」，「你要我打你呀？」

問問題

» "Where is the library?" she asked.

她問，「圖書館在哪裡？」

» Can I ask you a question?

我可以問你一個問題嗎？

» Go and ask Mary if she can come.

去問瑪莉她能不能去。

» I asked Mary how she made it.

我問瑪莉，她怎麼做到的。

» I don't know the answer. I'll ask around about it.

我不知道答案，我會多方面打聽。

* ask around 是個片語，就是「多方面打聽」的意思。

請求幫忙

» If you need help, you have to **ask**.
如果你需要幫忙，你就得提出要求。

» **Ask** Mary to give you a ride.
去要求瑪莉載你。

» **Ask** your brother if we could use his computer.
去問你哥哥，我們可不可以用他的電腦。

要價

» How much did she **ask for** the diamond ring?
這顆鑽戒她要賣多少錢？

邀請

» Do you think it's okay for me to **ask** her **out**?
你想我邀她出去好嗎？

» He **asked** her **out** to dinner, but she had other plans.
他邀她去吃晚餐，但是她有其他的事。

13 answer

回答

» Did he answer your question?
他有沒有回答你的問題？

» You still haven't answered my question.
你還是沒有回答我的問題。

應門；接電話

» Shall I answer the phone?
你要我接電話嗎？

» Don't answer the door while your parents are not home.
你的父母不在的時候，不要應門。

» Will you answer the door?
你去應門好嗎？

回信

» Have you answered Mary's letter yet?
你給瑪莉回信了嗎？

>>> 14 <<<

call

叫

» What do you want to call the new puppy?

這隻小狗你要取什麼名字？

＊ call 在這裡是「取名字、命名」的意思。

» We'll have to call a cab if the rain doesn't stop soon.

如果雨不很快停的話，我們必須叫部計程車。

打電話

» I'll call you later.

我稍後再打電話給你。

» She will call us from the airport when she arrives.

她到的時候，會從機場打電話給我們。

» I think we should call the doctor.

我認為我們應該打電話給醫生。

» If you don't leave, I'll call the police.

如果你不離開的話，我要叫警察。

其它的用法

» My English teacher calls the roll every day.

我的英文老師每天都點名。

＊ call the roll 就是「點名」的意思。

慣用語特好用

call on

» We called on Mary last week.

我們上星期去拜訪瑪莉。

＊ call on 是「拜訪某人」的意思。

call back

» I'll call you back.

我會再打電話給你。

» Can you ask Mary to call me back when she gets in?

瑪莉回來的時候，請她回我電話。

* call back 是「打電話回去給某人」的意思。

call someone names

» He called me names again.

他又在罵我。

* call 某人 names，就是用難聽的話罵那個人，例如：罵他笨蛋、白痴或是其他不好聽的話。

call in sick

» John called in sick this morning.

約翰今天早上打電話來請病假。

* call in sick 就是「打電話去請病假」的意思。

>>>

call for

» The forecast **calls for** more rain.

氣象預報說還會繼續下雨。

＊call for 就是「說天氣可能會…」的意思。

口語特常說

call it a day

你在公司上班，當你決定該回家了，你就可以說這句話，如果大家一起收工，你可以說 Let's call it a day.；如果你想下班先走，可以說，I'm going to call it a day.

聽到聲音

» Did you **hear** that strange noise?
你有沒有聽到那奇怪的噪音？

» My grandmother doesn't **hear** well.
我的祖母聽不太清楚。

» Did you **hear** the baby crying?
你有沒有聽到嬰孩在哭？

» She faintly **heard** the telephone ringing in the kitchen.
她微微聽到廚房裡電話鈴響著。

» I **heard** him walking down the stairs.
我聽到他走下樓。

» I'm sorry, I didn't hear what you said.
對不起，我沒聽到你說什麼。

hear 可以當「有人告訴你一些事情」的意思

» I hear what you are saying, but I disagree.

我懂得你的意思，但是我不同意。

* hear 在這裡是「聽懂你的意思」或「聽到你的意見」的意思。

» I'm sorry to hear that.

聽到那件事，我很難過。

» I'm glad to hear that you are getting better.

聽到你好多了，我很高興。

聽說

» I hear you're quitting the job.

我聽說你要辭職。

» I hear prices are going up.

我聽說價錢上漲了。

» I heard that John was fired.

我聽說約翰被開除。

» Did you hear about the accident?
你有沒有聽說那件車禍的消息？

» I've heard a lot about you.
我常常聽到你的事情。

» Have you heard anything of John lately?
你有沒有約翰最近的消息？

» What do you hear from your brother in America?
你哥哥在美國，寄信來說些什麼事？
* hear from 是個片語，是「收到消息」或「收到對方寄來的信」的意思。

其它的用法

» The judge will hear the case on May 10.
法官五月十日要審理這個案子。
* hear 在這裡是「審理案子」的意思。

慣用語特好用

hear of someone

» I've heard of John Lin, but I've never met him.

我聽過林約翰這個人，但是我從未見過他。

hear from someone

» Have you heard from John?

約翰有沒有跟你聯絡？

* hear from 某人，就是說「你有某人的消息」。

hear about

» Did you hear about Mary?

你聽說瑪莉的事嗎？

* hear about 是「得知某人發生的事」。

口語特常說

Do you hear me?

Do you hear me? 這句口語，是用在你要確定對方有聽到你說的話，而且也明白你在說什麼的時候，尤其是你在命令對方做什麼事情的時候。

I've heard so much about you.

當有人介紹某個人跟你認識時，你說 I've heard so much about you. 這句話表示，這個介紹你們兩個認識的人，常跟你提起對方。

16 turn

轉身；轉動某個東西

» He **turned** and ran away.
他轉身跑開。

» **Turn around** and face me.
轉過來，面對著我。

» She **turned** to look back at him as she got on the train.
當她上火車的時候，轉過來看他。

» **Turn** to the left.
轉到左邊。

» **Turn** to page 10.
翻到第十頁。

» The milk turned sour.
牛奶變酸。

» The leaves turn color in the fall.
樹葉在秋天變顏色。

» The clothes all turned pink in the wash.
衣服在洗的時候，通通變成粉紅色。

» She turned red when John teased her.
約翰取笑她的時候，她臉上變紅。

» Her hair is starting to turn gray.
她的頭髮開始變成灰色。

慣用語特好用

turn in

- It's late. I think I'll turn in.
  很晚了。我要去睡覺了。
  ＊turn in 就是「上床睡覺」的意思。

- Did you turn in your paper yet?
  你的報告交了沒有？
  ＊ turn in 也可以當「交某樣東西給某人」的意思。

turn off

- Please turn off the lights when you leave.
  你要離開的時候，請把燈關掉。

turn on

- What time are the street lights turned on?
  街燈幾點開？

turn out

- I hope everything turns out all right.
  我希望結果還令人滿意。
  ＊ turn out 就是「結果是」的意思。

17 drop

掉下來

» Ripe fruit dropped from the trees.
熟的水果從樹上掉下來。

» He dropped his pen.
他的筆掉到地上。

» Mary accidentally dropped her plant from the window.
瑪莉不小心把她的花從窗戶掉下去。

» I must have dropped my keys in the bus this morning.
我的鑰匙一定是今早掉在公車上。

停止；結束

» Let's drop the subject.
我們不要談這個話題。

» You should drop everything and take a vacation.
你應該放下一切，去度假。

降低（聲音、價錢、氣溫）

» They dropped their voices as they went into the library.
他們進了圖書館，就把聲音放低。

» The temperature will drop below zero tonight.
今晚氣溫會降到零下。

» The stock market dropped today.
今天股市下跌。

» House prices have dropped sharply lately.
最近房價跌得很厲害。

» The unemployment rate has dropped.

失業率已經下降。

» The wind speed has dropped.

風勢已減弱。

拜訪

» Drop by whenever you are in the town.

你到本市來的時候，要過來坐坐。

» Please drop in when you get a chance.

你有空，就過來坐坐。

» We would love you to drop over some time.

我們喜歡你有空過來坐坐。

＊在以上三句話裡，drop by，drop in 和 drop over 這三個片語都是「到某人家坐坐」，也就是「沒有什麼特別的事，到某人家拜訪一下」的意思。

其它的意思

» Drop me a note when you get there.

你到的時候，給我寫封信。

＊ drop 在這裡是「寄信給某人」的意思。

» Could you drop me off at my house?

你可以載我到我家嗎？

＊ drop 在這裡是「載某人到某個地方」的意思。

» I wish I hadn't dropped piano lessons.

我希望我沒有停掉鋼琴課。

＊ drop 在這裡的意思是「停止上某一門課」，也就是 stop taking 的意思。

慣用語特好用

drop out

» She dropped out of school.

她輟學了。

口語特常說

Drop in sometime.

Drop in sometime. 這句話是邀請對方，有空過來你家坐坐，或是跟對方說，若是他正好到你家附近時，請進來坐坐。英語會話裡有其他的說法，例如：Drop by sometime. 或 Drop by for a drink. 或 Drop over sometime. 都是表達同樣的意思。

Drop me a note.

當有朋友要遠行時，你會叫他，記得跟你寫信，以便保持聯繫，英語的說法就是，Drop me a note. 或 Drop me a line.

18

carry

拿；運送

» Will you carry my bag, please?
請你幫我拿袋子。

» The large pipe carries water.
這條大的管子是輸送水用的。

» Air carries sound.
空氣能傳聲音。

刊登；電視播放

» All the newspapers carried the news of their divorce.
所以的報紙都刊登他們離婚的消息。
＊ carry 在這裡是「刊登」的意思。

» He watched the football game, carried live on ABC.

他看由美國廣播公司實況轉播的足球賽。

＊ carry 在這裡是「電視播放」的意思。

有保險、有保證

» Do you carry any life insurance?

你有保人壽保險嗎？

» That car carries a four-year warranty.

那部車子有四年的保證。

carry 的其他用法

» Many serious diseases are carried by mosquitoes.

很多嚴重的疾病是蚊子傳染的。

＊ carry 在這裡是「傳送疾病」的意思。

» The suitcase can carry enough clothes for two weeks.

這個皮箱裝的下兩個星期需要的衣服。

＊ carry 在這裡是「容納（物件、酒量）等」的意思。

>>>

» How much weight will this bridge carry?

這座橋的載重量是多少？

＊ carry 在這裡是「支撐」的意思。

» Although she carries her age well, she must be over fifty.

雖然她不顯老，但是她應該已超過五十歲。

＊ carry one's age well 就是「不顯老」的意思。

» Does your store carry black skirts?

你們店裡有賣黑色的裙子嗎？

＊ carry 也可以做「商店有賣某樣東西」的意思。

» She always carries her purse.

她總是帶著她的皮包。

» Do you carry a pen?

你有沒有帶筆？

＊ carry 在以上兩句話裡的意思是「帶在身上」。

» Sometimes her brother carries his teasing too far and makes her cry.

有時候她的哥哥玩笑開得太過火，而把她弄哭。

＊ carry 在這裡的意思是「繼續做某件事」。

» Mary's opinions carry a lot of weight with the management.
瑪莉的意見對主管們很有影響力。

» Such a crime carries twenty-five years to life in that country.
這種罪，在那個國家會處二十五年有期徒刑至無期徒刑。

慣用語特好用

carry the ball

- John can't carry the ball. He isn't organized enough.
  不可以讓約翰負責。他不夠有條理。
  * carry the ball 就是「負責」的意思。

carry out

- Do you think you can carry out the job?
  你認為你能完成這個工作嗎？
  * carry out 是「完成任務」或「完成指定作業」的意思。

賣

» I'll sell you my car for $2000.

我的車子要賣兩千元。

» If I offer you another hundred, will you sell?

如果我多出一百元，你要賣嗎？

» John is selling his car for $1000.

約翰的車子要賣一千元。

» Do you sell boots?

你們有賣馬靴嗎？

* 這句話用在，問商店有沒有賣某樣東西。

» His new book sold well.

他的新書賣得很好。

» They will sell their house to anyone who will pay $100,000 for it.

有人願意出十萬元買他們的房子，他們就會賣。

慣用語特好用

sell something short

- This is a very good movie. Don't sell it short.

  這是一部好電影。別低估它。

  * sell something short 就是「低估某件事情」的意思。

sell someone out

- You'll be sorry if you sell him out.

  如果你出賣他的話，你會後悔。

  * sell 某人 out 就是「出賣某人」的意思。

sell out

- All the tickets are sold out.

  所有的票都賣光了。

  * sell out 在這裡是「賣光」的意思。

20

buy

買

» Where can I buy an antique desk?

我在哪裡可以買到古董書桌？

» I bought this lamp for $10 at the sale.

我在打折的時候用十塊錢買到這個燈。

» A dollar doesn't buy much these days.

這年頭一塊錢買不到什麼東西。

不相信

» Don't give me that excuse. I don't buy it.

別跟我說那個理由。我不相信。

賄賂

» They say the judge was bought.

聽說法官已經被收買了。

請客

» Let me buy you a drink.

我請你喝一杯。

慣用語特好用

buy someone off

- John tried to buy off the cops.

  約翰想要買通警員。

buy something out

- They thought the company was badly run, so they bought it out.

  他們認為這家公司經營不善，所以他們把它買下來。

  * buy something out 就是「全部買下來」或「整個買下來」的意思。

21

get

收到；得到

» I got a computer for my birthday.
我收到一部電腦做我的生日禮物。

» Where can I get a good haircut?
哪裡剪頭髮剪的好？

» Where did you get that antique desk?
你在哪裡買到那個古董書桌？

» I got this vase at the flea market.
我在跳蚤市場買到這個花瓶。

» I got a busy signal.
對方電話有人在使用。
＊打電話時，如果對方電話正在使用，你就會聽到「使

用中」的信號。

» How much are you expecting to get for your car?

你這部車打算賣多少錢？

去；到達

» How long will it take to get to the beach?

到海邊要多久？

» It takes me five hours to get home from here.

從這裡回到家要五小時。

» It's going to take twenty minutes to get to the movies from John's house.

從約翰家到戲院需要二十分鐘。

get 當連綴動詞，後面要接形容詞，例如：get

» This is getting ridiculous.

這越來越荒唐。

» Eat your dinner before it gets cold.
在飯冷前快吃。

» It's getting hot in here.
這裡面越來越熱。

» John and Susan are getting married in June.
約翰和蘇珊六月要結婚。

» Get out of the rain or you'll get wet.
不要待在雨中，否則你會淋濕。

擁有

» What kind of car has your brother got?
你哥哥開什麼樣的車子？

» John's got a Master's Degree in History.
約翰擁有歷史的碩士學位。

瞭解；聽得懂

» Did you get the joke?
你聽得懂這個笑話嗎？

» He just didn't get it.

他就是聽不懂。

* 聽不懂別人說的笑話。

其它用法

» Such bad habits will get you finally.

這種壞習慣會害了你。

» Did you get the look on his face?

你有沒有注意到他臉上的表情？

* get 在這裡是「注意到」的意思。

» The ball got him on the head.

球打到他的頭上。

* get 在這裡是「打」的意思。

» I couldn't get to sleep.

我睡不著。

» When Mary got the news, she passed out.

當瑪莉聽到這個消息的時候，她就昏倒。

* get 在這裡是「得到消息」的意思。

慣用語特好用

get up

» What time do you usually get up?

你通常都幾點起床？

＊ get up 就是「起床」的意思。

get together

» It's good to see you, Mary. We'll have to get together again.

瑪莉，很高興見到你。我們應該再聚一聚。

＊ get together 就是「朋友相聚」的意思。

get through

» When can you get through the assignment I gave you?

我交給你的作業你何時可以做完？

＊ get through 就是「做完」的意思。

口語特常說

Let me get this straight.

Let me get this straight. 這句話是用在，你要跟對方確定一下，你沒聽錯對方的意思，例如：明天是放假日，但是你的老闆要你來上班，你要確定你沒聽錯，他的確叫你明天來上班，你就先說一句 Let me get this straight. 再問你的老闆說，你的意思是叫我明天要來上班。

Get lost.

Get lost. 大家都學過的，就是「迷路」的意思，但是 Get lost! 還有另一個用法，就是當你覺得某個人很煩，你要叫他走開，或是叫他別再煩你，你也可以叫他 Get lost!

22

see

看

» I can't see a thing without my glasses.

我不戴眼鏡看不到東西。

» Did you see the sign?

你有沒有看到牌子？

» I saw a turtle as I was going to work this morning.

今早我要去上班的時候，看到一隻烏龜。

查看

» Can I see your ticket?

請把票拿給我看。

» Go and see if the oven is off.

去看看火爐有沒有關。

瞭解

» I can see that you're angry.

我看得出你在生氣。

» Mary looks very tired. I can see why.

瑪莉看起來很累。我知道為什麼。

» Do you see what I mean?

你知道我的意思嗎？

＊ see 在這裡是「瞭解別人說的話」的意思。

» Do you see the point of the joke?

你聽得懂這個笑話在說什麼嗎？

再見

» See you later.

再見。

» I'll be seeing you.

再見。

» See you around.

再見。

見面；拜訪

» I want to see Mr. Lin.

我要見林先生。

» When you are in the town, come to see us.

你到本市來的時候，過來看我們。

» We're going to see Mary. Do you want to come along?

我們要去看瑪莉，你要不要一起來？

» I saw Mary at the post office this morning.

今天早上我在郵局遇到瑪莉。

* see 在這裡是「無意中遇見」的意思。

» She doesn't want to see anyone at the moment.

她此刻不想見任何人。

* see 在這裡是「會客」的意思。

» I heard John is seeing another woman.

我聽說約翰在跟另一個女人交往。

* see 在這裡是「與別人幽會」的意思。

» You should go see a doctor.

你應該去看醫生。

想像

» I can't see him objecting to it.

我不認為他會反對這件事。

確定

» See that the door is locked

要確定門有上鎖。

經歷

» Our town has seen many changes.

我們鎮上已經改變很多。

送行

» I'll see you to the door.

我送你到門口。

» Do you need me to see you back to the dorm?

你要我送你回宿舍嗎？

» I'll be back as soon as I see Mary home.

我送瑪莉回家之後，會馬上回來。

慣用語特好用

see someone off

- We went to the airport to see Mary off.

  我們到機場給瑪莉送行。

  * see 某人 off，就是「去給某人送行」。

see the last of someone

- They are happy to see the last of John.

  他們很高興以後不會再看到約翰。

＊ see the last of 某人，就是「最後一次看到他，以後不會再看到他了」。

see to something

- I hear the doorbell. Will someone **see to the door**?

  我聽到門鈴聲，有沒有人要去應門？

  ＊ see to 某件事，就是「照料一下這件事」。

口語特常說

See you!

See you! 是用在跟別人道別，而你知道你還會再見到對方時。

See you later.

See you later. 是跟對方說「待會兒見」，也就是你跟對方道別，但是你很快就會再見到他。

See you around.

See you around. 是跟對方道別，但是沒有約什麼時候會再見面。

23

watch

看

» Do you want to **watch** TV at home or go to the movies?

你要在家裡看電視，還是去看電影？

＊看電視的英語是 watch TV，看報紙的英語是 read the newspaper，而去看電影則是說 go to the movies。

» They are **watching** the football game.

他們在看足球賽。

» She **watched** the children play in the playground.

她看著小朋友在遊樂場遊玩。

» **Watch** carefully while I show you how to run the computer.

我教你如何用電腦的時候，你要用心看。

小心

» Watch that you don't drop the camera.
小心照相機不要摔了。

照料；看管

» Can you watch the kids while I am away?
我不在的時候，你可以看著孩子們嗎？

» The lifeguard watched the children while they played in the swimming pool.
當小孩子在游泳池遊玩的時候，救生員在看著。

慣用語特好用

watch for

» The man watched for his bus to arrive.
這個人在等他的公車到。

24

look

看

» Look at the sunset.

你看夕陽。

» Look, there's a deer.

你看，有一隻鹿。

» If you look carefully, you'll see what's wrong.

如果你仔細看，你就會看出錯在哪裡。

» Sorry, I didn't see. I was looking somewhere else.

對不起，我沒看到。我剛剛在看別的地方。

» John looked at his watch and said, "It's

late.".
約翰看他的手錶，說「很晚了」。

找

» We looked everywhere but we couldn't find it.
我們到處都找過了，但是找不到。

» Have you looked under the sofa?
沙發椅底下你找過了嗎？

» Did you look in every pocket for the keys?
找鑰匙，你每一個口袋都找過了嗎？

» What are you looking for?
你在找什麼？

» I'm looking for the remote control.
我在找遙控器。

似乎

» Mary looks sad.
瑪莉好像不太高興。

» He look tired after the business trip.
出差回來後，他看起來很累。

» How do I look in this dress?
我穿這件洋裝好不好看？

面向

» Our house looks east, so we get the sun first thing in the morning.
我們的房子向東，所以早上就有太陽照進來。

» The hotel looks toward the sea.
這間旅館面向大海。

» I like houses that look south.
我喜歡向南的房子。

» Our living room looks south.
我們的客廳向南。

查看

» I'll have to look at his medical history.
我必須要看看他的醫療記錄。

» She wanted the doctor to look at her arms.
她要醫生檢查她的手臂。

» The accountant looked closely at his financial records.
會計師很仔細的看他的財務記錄。

對事情的看法

» You'll look at things differently when you're older.
當你年紀大一點以後，看事情就會有不同。

在你要跟對方說話之前，先說 Look，這只是在用來讓對方知道你有話要說，在你說完 Look 這個字之後，接下來要說的，可能是表示「你有話要商量」、「你有不滿意的話要說」、「你要諷刺對方」或是表示「你的態度很堅決」或是「表示安慰」的意思。

» Look, can't we talk about it?
哪，我們不能談一談嗎？

» Look, I've had enough of this.
嘿，我已經受夠了。

» Look, I didn't mean to.
嘿，我不是故意的。

» Look, we all make mistakes.
嘿，誰不會犯錯。

慣用語特好用

look for trouble

- You are looking for trouble if you cheat in the exam.
  如果你考試作弊，那你是在自找麻煩。

look like

- It looks like it might rain.
  看起來好想要下雨。

look as if

- There are no buses so it looks as if we'll be walking home.
  沒有公車了，看起來我們要用走路回家。
- You look as if you haven't slept all night.

你看起來好像整晚沒睡。

look forward to

- We all look forward to your new book on cooking.
  我們都在期待你有關烹飪的新書。

Look out!

- Look out! There's a car coming.
  小心，有一部車子來了。

口語特常說

Look who's here.

Look who's here. 是在某個場合遇到熟人，或是有人沒有事先通知，就來拜訪你們時，你表示驚喜的說，「看看是誰來了」。

I'm just looking.

當你到商店或百貨公司逛時，若有店員前來問你，May I help you? 時，你就可以回答她說，I'm just looking. 或 I'm only looking. 表示你只是隨便逛逛。

25 find

找到

» I hope we can find a parking lot.
我希望我們找得到停車的地方。

» Could you find me a nice second-hand car?
你能不能替我找一部好的二手車？

» We found the solution to this problem.
我們找到解決這個問題的方法。

» Will we ever find a cure for cancer?
我們找得到治療癌症的方法嗎？

» We found a really good restaurant near the hotel.
我們在旅館附近找到一家很好的餐廳。

» I wouldn't mind helping you, but I can't find the time right now.
我不介意幫你的忙，但是我現在沒時間。

» Will you be able to find your way to my office?
到我辦公室的路，你找得到嗎？

發現

» When I got to the classroom, I found that class was cancelled.
我到教室的時候，才發現該堂課取消了。
＊find 在這裡是「到了的時候才知道」的意思。

» She finds that she can lose weight just by eating less.
她發現只要少吃點，她的體重就可以減輕。

慣用語特好用

find out

• I just found out our library books are overdue.
我剛發現我們跟圖書館借的書過期了。
＊find out 是「發現事實」的意思。

開始

» Let's start the computer lessons in June.
我們六月開始電腦課吧。

» You'd better start getting dressed soon.
你最好趕快開始穿衣服。

» Spring break starts on April 2.
春假四月二號開始。

» I've just started learning English.
我剛開始學英語。

» He started to cry.
他開始哭。

» The show starts at 7:30.
表演七點三十分開始。

» Have you started that book yet?
你開始看那本書了嗎？

» You'll have to start early to get to Chicago before nightfall.
你們得早點開始，才能在天黑之前到芝加哥。

» My son is starting school in September.
我兒子九月要開始上學。
* start 在這裡是「開始上學」的意思。

» I got a job and will start next week.
我找到工作，下星期開始上班。
* start 在這裡是「開始上班」的意思。

車子發動

» The car just won't start.
車子就是發不動。

» I couldn't get my car started this morning.

今天早上，我的車子不能發動。

其它用法

» He quit his job and started his own business last year.
他去年辭掉工作，開始他自己的事業。

» John started his own publishing business last year.
約翰去年開始他自己的出版事業。

» Mary always starts the day with a cup of coffee.
瑪莉早上總是要喝一杯咖啡。

開始

» We began to wonder if the bus would ever arrive.

我們開始懷疑公車是否會來。

» I began working in my present job two years ago.

我兩年前開始在目前這個工作上班。

» I'd like to begin by thanking you all for being here tonight.

我首先要謝謝你們今晚來這裡。

» The party begins at 7:30.

宴會七點半開始。

» My cold began with a sore throat.

我的感冒從喉嚨痛開始。

have

有

» Do you **have** any questions?
你有問題嗎？

» We **had** a good time at Mary's party.
我們在瑪莉的宴會玩得很愉快。

» She **has** blonde hair and blue eyes.
她有金黃色的頭髮，藍色的眼睛。

» How many pages does the book **have**?
這本書有幾頁？

» She **has** an idea on how to make the plan work.
要如何使這個計畫作得成，她有一個主意。

生病

» I had a cold.
我感冒了。

» My brother might have the chicken pox.
我弟弟可能是在長水痘。

have 當使役動詞

» I had my house painted last week.
上星期我叫人把房子油漆過。

» Where do you usually have your hair cut?
你通常在哪裡剪頭髮？

吃；喝

» She sat down and had another drink.
她坐下，再喝一杯。

» We usually have dinner at 7:00.
我們通常在七點吃晚飯。

>>>

想要某樣飲料或點心

» I'll have the apple pie for dessert, please.

我的點心要蘋果派。

» I'll have coffee.

我要咖啡。

慣用語特好用

have a crush on someone

- John has a crush on Mary

約翰愛上瑪莉。

* have a crush on 某人，就是「愛上某人」的意思。

have a fit

- John had a fit when he found his car had been damaged.

當約翰發現他的車子被撞壞時，他很生氣。

* have a fit 就是「很生氣」的意思。

have a word with

- Mary, can I have a word with you?

  瑪莉，我可以私下跟你談談嗎？

have cold feet

- I can't give my speech now. I have cold feet.

  我現在沒辦法演講。我會害怕。

  * have cold feet 就是「感到害怕」的意思。

>>> 29 <<<

catch

抓到

» The police didn't catch the thief.

警察沒有抓到小偷。

» We caught a rabbit.

我們抓到一隻兔子。

» The sleeve of his coat got caught on the door handle.

他的大衣袖子被門把鉤住。

趕上

» We will have to hurry to catch the train.

我們要快一點才能趕上火車。

» John started to run, and Mary could not catch him.
約翰開始跑，瑪莉趕不上他。

» I have to catch the 3:00 flight to New York.
我要去趕三點的飛機到紐約。

無意中發現

» The teacher caught John cheating at the exam.
老師抓到約翰考試作弊。

得到

» You'd better put on a coat, or you'll catch a cold.
你最好穿上大衣，否則你會感冒。

» I catch a cold every winter.
我每年冬天都感冒。

慣用語特好用

catch someone red-handed

- John tried to cheat at the exam, and the teacher **caught him red-handed**.

  約翰在考試時，想要作弊，被老師當場抓到。

  ＊ catch 某人 red-handed，就是「當某人正在做壞事時，當場被抓到」。

catch up

- If you miss a lot of lessons, it's very difficult to **catch up**.

  如果你有很多課沒上，很難趕得上。

  ＊ catch up 是「趕上」的意思。

30 break

打破

» Who broke the vase?

誰打破這個花瓶？

» The thief broke a window and got into the house.

小偷打破窗戶，進去屋子裡。

» Be careful not to break the glass.

小心不要打破玻璃。

» She fell off the bicycle and broke her arm.

她從腳踏車上摔下來，摔斷手臂。

» The seal on the jar was broken.

罐子上的封口破了。

>>>

把東西弄壞，使它不能用

» Someone's broken my camera.

有人把我的照相機弄壞了。

» John broke all the toys he got.

約翰把所有他拿得到的玩具都弄壞。

» The TV broke. Could you have someone fix it?

電視壞了，你能叫人來修理嗎？

» The boy will break the typewriter if he bangs on it.

如果這個男孩用力敲打字機的話，會把它弄壞。

其它的用法

» The dam finally broke, and the waters flooded the town.

水壩終於毀了，水淹沒這個城鎮。

* break 在這裡是「毀壞」的意思。

» Let's break for lunch now.

我們休息，吃午飯。

＊ break 在這裡是「休息」的意思。

» The mayor came to break ground for the new building.

市長來為新的大樓破土。

＊ break ground 是個片語，是「建築物施工前破土」。

» You'll break the law if you drive without a driver's license.

如果你沒有駕駛執照開車，你會觸犯法律。

» She never breaks a promise

她從來沒有食言。

» She hopes to break the school record at the entrance examination.

她希望破學校入學考試的紀錄。

慣用語特好用

break up

- John and Mary broke up.

  約翰和瑪莉兩個人不再來往。

break in

- Someone broke in and stole Mary's jewelry.

  有人闖空門，偷走瑪莉的珠寶。

  ＊ break in 就是「進去某人家或某個地方偷東西」。

MP3-32

31

care

在乎；關心

» He doesn't care what people think of him.
他不在乎人們對他的看法。

» I don't care whether we win or not.
我不在乎我們會不會贏。

» She cares about the quality of her work.
她在乎她工作的品質。

» I really care about him.
我真的很關心他。
＊ care about 是個片語，是「關心」的意思。

» She cares nothing about your money.
她並不在乎你的錢。

想要

» Would you care to go to the movies with me?
你要不要跟我去看電影？

» I really don't care to see that movie.
我真的不想去看那部電影。

» Would you care for a drink?
你要喝什麼飲料嗎？
＊ care for 這個片語，也可以做「想要」的意思。

喜歡

» I like Chinese food.
我喜歡中國菜。

» How do you like Taipei?
你喜歡台北嗎？

» I like your shoes.
我喜歡你的鞋子。
＊這句話就是說，「你的鞋子很好看」的意思。

» Do you like to swim?
你喜歡游泳嗎？

» I didn't like the way he talked to me.
我不喜歡他對我說話的方式。

» John doesn't like anyone talking back to

him.
約翰不喜歡別人回嘴。

» I'd like you to be honest with me.
我希望你對我誠實。

要什麼樣的

» How do you like your steak?
你要幾分熟的牛排？

» How do you like your coffee?
你的咖啡要不要加糖或奶精？

較喜歡；同意；偏袒

» The umpire seemed to **favor** the other team.

裁判好像偏袒另一隊。

» The mother **favors** her youngest son among all her children.

這個母親在她所有小孩中，最喜歡小兒子。

有助於；有利於

» The dark night **favored** his escape.

黑暗有助於他的逃跑。

» The new tax bill **favors** the rich people.

這個新稅法對有錢人有利。

長得比較像誰

» She **favors** her aunt Mary.

她長得像她的姑媽瑪莉。

» I **favor** my father side.

我像我爸爸那一邊。

34

keep

留著

» If you like the book, you can keep it.

如果你喜歡這本書，你可以留著。

＊ keep 在這裡的意思是「留著，不用還」的意思。

» I kept $200 for myself and gave him $50.

我自己留兩百元，給他五十元。

» We want to keep the old car.

這部舊車我們想要留著。

＊ keep 在這裡是「留著，不賣掉」的意思。

保持；繼續

» Try to keep the balance.

想辦法保持平衡。

» He keeps telling me the same story.
他一直告訴我同一個故事。

» I don't know what's keeping him.
我不知道什麼事絆住他。

» She kept her trim figure.
她保持苗條的身材。

» The teacher asked the class to keep quiet.
老師要求班上保持安靜。

» Come closer to the fireplace. It'll keep you warm.
來火爐邊，可以使你保持暖和。

把東西放在某個地方

» She keeps her jewelry in a safe.
她把她的珠寶放在保險櫃。

» He keeps his money in a savings account.

他的錢存在儲蓄帳號。

» I always keep an umbrella in the car.

我總是放一把傘在車上。

使維持

» She kept a diary of what she did every day.

她有一本日記，記她每天作的事。

» Can I trust you to keep a secret?

我可以信任你會守祕密嗎？

» The refrigerator keeps meat fresh.

冰箱使肉保持新鮮。

其它用法

» The weather may keep the plants from budding.

這種氣候，植物可能不會萌芽。

* keep 在這裡是「防止」的意思。

» We all help my mother keep house.

我們都幫助媽媽整理屋子。

＊ keep 在這裡是「照料、整理」的意思。

慣用語特好用

keep in touch

» I hope we can **keep in touch**.

我希望我們能保持聯繫。

試著做某件事

» We must **try** to help them.
我們必須試著幫助他們。

» You must **try** to control your temper.
你必須試著控制你的脾氣。

» He **tried** moving the bookshelf alone, but it was too heavy.
他試著自己移動書架，但是書架太重了。

» I'll **try** not to be late again.
我會試著不要再遲到。

» She may not be good at singing, but at least she **tries**.
她可能不會唱歌，但是至少她試了。

>>>

做試驗；嘗試

» Scientists are trying the new drugs on rats.

科學家在老鼠身上試驗新的藥。

» Mary likes to try anything new.

瑪莉喜歡嘗試新的東西。

試試看

» If you want to buy an old lamp, try garage sale.

如果你想買個舊燈，到「車庫拍賣」試試看。

＊ try 在這裡的意思是，有人要買某樣東西，你叫他到某個地方看看，那兒可能會有。

» Try John. He may know how to do it.

問問約翰，他或許知道如何做。

＊ try 在這裡的意思是，當有人有問題時，你建議他，去問某人看看，他或許知道。

» Why don't you try Mary? Maybe she can give you a ride.

你何不問瑪麗看看？或許她會載你。

＊ try 在這裡的意思是，對方想找人載他，你建議他，去

問瑪莉看看，或許她會載對方。

» Could you try again later?
你稍後再試試看好嗎？

» Try the other door. It may not be locked.
試試另一扇門，它或許沒上鎖。

試吃某樣東西看喜不喜歡吃

» Have you tried this dish?
你有沒有嚐過這道菜？

» You must try that dish.
那一道菜你一定要嚐嚐看。

» Here, try this lemonade.
喏，嚐嚐這杯檸檬汁。

審訊

» John was tried for murder and found guilty.
約翰以謀殺罪被審判，而且被判有罪。

慣用語特好用

try on

- Did you try it on before you bought it?

  你買之前有沒有試穿？

  ＊try on 就是「試穿」的意思。

放

» Put those books on the shelf.

把那些書放在架子上。

» Where did you put the keys?

你把鑰匙放在哪裡？

» You put too much salt in the soup.

你在湯裡放太多鹽。

» They put him on the second shift.

他們把他排在小夜班。

使某人處在某種情況之中

» The news has put us in a bad mood.

這個消息讓我們的心情變糟。

» The sound of the waves put me to sleep.
海浪的聲音催我入眠。

» The doctor put him in the emergency room.
醫生把他放在急診室裡。

說法

» Put your question clearly.
把你的問題說清楚。

» Can you put your problem in simple words?
你簡單地描述你的問題嗎？

其它的用法

» We have to put a stop to cheating.
我們必須阻止作弊。
* put 在這裡的說法也可以用，put an end to 某件事。

» He puts his family first.
他把他的家庭放在第一位。

» Put your name at the top of each answer sheet.
把你的名字寫在每張答案紙的上端。

» I hope you like it. I've put so much time into it.
我希望你喜歡。我已經花了很多時間去做。

慣用語特好用

put on

- It's cold outside. You'd better put on your coat.
外面很冷。你最好穿上大衣。
＊put on 是「穿上衣服」的意思。

put off

- The meeting has been put off until

tomorrow.

會議延期到明天。

＊ put off 是「延期」的意思。

put in

- I've **put in** a lot of effort to have it done.

  我很努力，把這件事做完。

  ＊ put in 就是「花時間精神去做某件事情」。

遊玩

» She watched the children play in the playground.

她看著小孩子在遊樂場玩耍。

» Mary played a trick on John.

瑪莉捉弄約翰。

» Don't play with matches.

不要玩火柴。

打球

» Do you like to play golf?

你喜歡打高爾夫球嗎？

» We won't be ready to play against the other team this weekend.

這個週末我們還不能跟另一隊打。

» They are not competing. They are playing for practice.

他們不是在比賽。他們是在練習。

播放音樂；彈奏樂器

» John likes to play the radio when he studies.

約翰在讀書的時候，喜歡開著收音機。

» I've always wanted to learn to play the violin.

我一直想學拉小提琴。

» I could hear a flute playing Christmas songs next door.

我可以聽到隔壁，長笛吹奏著聖誕歌曲。

表演

» I'd like to play Snow White.

我要飾演白雪公主。

* play 在這裡是「演戲時飾演某一個角色」的意思。

» "Cats" is playing at the Majesty Theater now.

「貓」這齣音樂劇現在在皇家戲院上演。

* play 在這裡是「某一個戲劇在上演」的意思。

假裝

» Don't play dumb in the principal's office.

在校長辦公室裡別裝傻。

扮演角色；起作用；有影響

» He played a huge part in yesterday's football game.

他對昨天的足球賽有很大的影響。

出牌

» She couldn't decided which card to play.

她沒辦法決定要出那一張牌。

慣用語特好用

play with

» Stop playing with the light switch.

不要玩電燈開關。

＊ play with 某樣東西，就是「一直去動那樣東西」的意思。

>>> 38 <<<

pass

經過

» We passed each other on the staircase.
我們在樓梯間，錯身而過。

» Many cars have passed us, but none of them was John's.
已經有很多部車子過去了，但是沒有一部是約翰的。

» I think we just passed Main street.
我想我們剛過了緬因街。

» We passed the post office on the way home from work yesterday.
昨天我們下班回家的路上經過郵局。

超過；趕過去

» He drove faster in order to pass the car in front of him on the highway.

他開得快些，以便趕過高速公路上在他前面的那一部車子。

» He passed the others in the 100-meter race.

在一百米賽跑中他超過其它的人。

走過；穿過

» She passed through the gate.

她走過大門。

» When I pass that store, I always look in the windows.

當我走過那家店的時候，我總是看看櫥窗。

河流流過

» A beautiful river passes through the city.

有一條漂亮的河流流經這個城市。

時間過去

» The days passed by quickly.

日子很快的過去。

» Several years passed before she got over the loss of her son .

到她能不再悲痛她兒子的去世，已經是好幾年以後的事了。

通過考試；通過測驗

» My car didn't pass inspection.

我的車子沒通過檢驗。

» I passed the English test.

我英文考及格了。

» Did John pass the driving test?

約翰有沒有通過路考？

通過法律

» Congress passed a series of important measures last year.

國會去年通過一連串重要的法案。

遞某樣東西給另一個人

» Pass the butter, please.

請把奶油遞過來。

» Can you pass me the dictionary?

把字典遞給我好嗎？

» Mary passed a note to Jane during class.

瑪莉在課堂上傳紙條給珍。

» Could you pass the card to John, please?

請你把卡片傳過去給約翰好嗎？

＊ 這句話用在你要拿東西給約翰，但是有人正好在你們兩個的中間，所以你就請這個中間人把東西遞給約翰。

傳佈消息

» Please pass along information about the meeting to anyone you see.

請把開會的消息告訴每個你遇到的人。

事情會過去

» The fever passed.

退燒了。

其它的用法

» The season passed slowly from fall to winter.

季節慢慢地由秋天變成冬天。

＊ pass 在這裡是「從一種情況轉變成另一種情況」的意思。

» The house will be passed on to her son when she dies.

她過世之後，房子會傳給她兒子。

＊ pass 在這裡是「所有權從一個人傳到另一個人」的意思。

慣用語特好用

pass out

» When Mary got the news, she passed out.

當瑪莉聽到這個消息的時候，她就昏倒。

＊ pass out 是「昏倒」的意思。

pass away

» His mother passed away last year.

他的母親去年過世。

＊ pass away 和 pass on 都是「逝世」的意思。

口語特常說

pass

當有人問你問題，而你不會，你可以說 pass，表示你不會，讓下一個人去回答，或是當你在玩撲克牌時，你這一次不出牌，你也可以說 pass，表示你不出牌，下一位可以繼續。

失敗；沒做成

» Peace talks between the two countries have failed.
兩國之間的和平談判失敗。

» Millions of people have tried to lose weight and failed.
已經有幾百萬人嘗試減肥卻失敗。

沒有做應該做的事

» John failed to take the final exam.
約翰沒有去考期末考。

» She failed to do the dishes for five days in a row.

她一連五天沒有洗碗。

» His parachute failed to open.
他的降落傘沒有張開。

» My grandchildren never fail to phone me on my birthday.
我生日那一天，我的孫子們從沒有忘記打電話給我。

考試不及格

» If you don't study hard, you'll fail the exam.
如果你不用功讀書，你會考不及格。

» He failed the driving test the first time he took it.
他第一次考路考的時候，沒考過。

公司生意失敗

» Many small business failed in the recession.
許多小生意在經濟不景氣時倒閉。

» The rocket's engine failed a few seconds after take-off.

火箭的引擎在發射後幾秒鐘，就發生故障。

農作物歉收

» The entire Idaho potato crop failed miserably this year.

整個愛達荷州的馬鈴薯今年嚴重歉收。

40

order

點菜；訂購

» Are you ready to order?

你可以點菜了嗎？

» She ordered the steak meal.

她點了牛排餐。

» I've ordered the book Mary wants to read.

我已經訂了那本瑪莉想要讀的書。

» We ordered eggs and bread from the grocery store.

我們在雜貨店訂購蛋和麵包。

» I ordered some books from a mail-order company.

我從一家郵購公司訂購一些書。

命令

» The policeman ordered the thief to put up his hands.
警察命令小偷把手舉起來。

» The commandant ordered them to line up against the wall.
指揮官命令他們靠著牆排好。

» The teacher ordered John out of the room.
老師命令約翰到教室外面去。

按次序排列

» The diamonds are ordered according to size.
鑽石按照尺寸大小排列。

» John ordered the books on the shelves.
約翰按次序把書在書架上排好。

work

上班

» John is 80, and still **working**.
約翰已經八十歲，還在上班。

» I **work** overtime a lot.
我常加班。

» There's no way I'm **working** Sundays.
我絕不在星期天上班。

» I've been **working** long hours lately.
最近我工作時間很長。

» Mary isn't **working** tomorrow.
瑪莉明天不上班。

» My sister works in a law firm.
我妹妹在一家律師事務所上班。

» Mary works in that office building.
瑪莉在那棟辦公大樓裡上班。

在某家公司上班

» She's been working for IBM for years now.
她已經在 IBM 上班多年。

» John works for Microsoft I believe.
約翰應該是在微軟公司上班。

» Mary works for either Nations Banks or Bank of America.
瑪莉不是在國家銀行就是在美國銀行上班。

» John works as a chemical engineer at Dupont.
約翰在杜邦公司擔任石化工程師。

做事情

» She's been working all day in the kitchen.

她已經在廚房裡忙了一整天。

機器運轉正常

» The telephone is not **working**.
電話壞了。

» My microwave has not been **working** since I bought it.
我的微波爐自從買回來以後，一直是壞的。

有效；行得通

» Will the plan **work**?
這個計畫行得通嗎？

» I don't think his idea will **work**.
我不認為他的主意行得通。

42

use

使用

» Can I use your computer?

我可以用你的電腦嗎？

＊這句話是用在「要向別人借東西使用時」，例如：你要借電話，就是 Can I use your phone?

» We use this room for storing old books.

我們用這個房間來儲藏舊書。

» She used her intelligence to solve problems.

她用她的聰明去解決問題。

＊use 在這裡是「使用、運用」的意思。

» What do you use to make your lawn so green?

你用什麼東西，使你的草地這麼青翠？

利用別人

» He uses others to do his dirty work for him.

他利用別人替他做非法的事。

特好用

use up

• Who used up the last of the toothpaste?

誰把牙膏通通用完？

＊ use up 某樣東西，就是「把那樣東西全部用玩」。

get used to

• Have you gotten used to the weather yet?

你適應這種天氣了嗎？

＊ get used to 和 be used to 都是「適應」的意思。

口語特常說

could use

如果你要搬家，朋友問你需要什麼嗎，你覺得你需要幫忙，你可以回答說 I could use a hand.，句子中的 could use 某樣東西的意思就是，你想要有這樣東西。

43

send

寄送；派遣；送某人到某個地方

» I'd like to send the letter by airmail.
我要用航空寄這封信。

» I'll send Mary a card to congratulate her.
我要寄一張卡片給瑪莉，跟她恭喜。

» Could you send up two glasses of orange juice?
請你派人送兩杯柳橙汁上來。
＊ 這句話是，你住旅館時，跟客房服務叫食物的用法。

» She sent John to buy some milk.
她派約翰去買牛奶。

» They sent their son to America to study .
他們把他們的兒子送到美國讀書。

>>>

對某人產生某種影響

» His rude remark sent her into a rage.
他無禮的話讓她很生氣。

» His boring speech sent me into sleep.
他乏味的演講，催我入睡。

慣用語特好用

send for

- Mary is ill. Please send for a doctor.
  瑪莉病了，請派人請醫生來。
  * send for 在這裡是「派人去請某人來」的意思。

- We'll have to send for another one.
  我們必須請對方再送另外一個來。
  * send for 也可以做「訂購某樣東西，請對方送來」。

send out for

- We are too busy to go out for lunch. Why not send out for sandwiches?
  我們太忙了，沒有時間去吃午飯。何不叫餐廳送外賣三明治過來？
  * send out for 是「請餐廳或飲食店送食物來」的意思。

知道

» Do you know when the train will arrive?
你知道火車什麼時候會到嗎？

» Give him this medicine, and let me know if he's not better in two days.
給他這個藥，兩天內他如果沒有好轉，通知我。

» I just know he won't let me do it.
我知道他不會讓我做。

» I knew you'd say that.
我知道你會這麼說。

» How do you know he'll finish it on time?
你怎麼知道他會準時做完？

» Mary **knows** how to use the accounting software.

瑪莉知道如何使用這個會計軟體。

* know 在這裡是「會某種技能」的意思。

» Do you **know** the people who live next door?

你認識住在隔壁的人嗎？

* know 在這裡是「認識」的意思。

» Do you **know** this song?

你知道這首歌嗎？

慣用語特好用

know something by heart

- I **know the song by heart**.

  這首歌我會背。

hold

» Can you hold the bags for me while I open the door?

我開門的時候，你可不可以替我拿著袋子？

» She held the baby in her arms.

她抱著嬰孩在手上。

» The couple held hands and sat at the beach.

這一對情侶手牽著手坐在海邊。

» Most of the management positions are held by men.

管理階層的職位大都是男士擔任。

＊ hold 在這裡是「擔任某一重要的職位」的意思。

>>>

保留某樣東西給某個人

» Will you hold "The Old Man and the Sea" for me?

請你替我把「老人與海」一書留著。

＊ 這句話是用在，你請圖書管理員幫你留著這本書，不要借出，所以你可以來借。

» They will hold a double room for us.

他們會為我們留一間雙人房。

擁有；持有

» He holds 10,000 shares of the company.

他擁有一萬股這個公司的股份。

容納；包含

» The auditorium holds 2000 people.

這座禮堂可容納兩千人。

» This box will hold all of my stuff.

這個盒子可以裝我所有的東西。

其它用法

» The judge held that he was at fault.

法官裁定是他的錯。

* hold 在這裡是「做出裁決」的意思。

» I don't think that chair will hold you.

我不認為那個椅子能夠支撐你。

* hold 在這裡是「支撐」的意思。

慣用語特好用

hold on

- Hold on. I'll go get her.

請稍候，我去叫她來聽電話。

hold one's breath

- How long can you hold your breath?

你能夠屏住呼吸多久？

* hold one's breath 是「摒住呼吸」的意思。

>>> 46 <<<

lose

失去

» I've lost a lot of weight.
我體重減輕很多。

» He can't afford to lose his job. He has a family to support.
他不能失去他的工作。他要養家。

» We're going to lose several salesmen.
我們會失去好幾個售貨員。

» I lost a lot of money in the stock market.
我在股票市場輸很多錢。

比賽輸了，選舉沒選上

» When I play tennis with Mary, I always lose.

我跟瑪莉打網球，我總是輸。

» Our team lost by ten points.

我們隊輸十分。

＊ lose 在以上兩句話裡，都是「在比賽時輸了」的意思。

» John lost the presidential election.

約翰選總統沒選上。

＊ lose 在這裡的意思是「選舉沒選上」。

找不到

» Make sure you don't lose each other in the crowd.

要確定你們不要在人群中走失了。

» I've lost my wallet.

我的皮包丟了。

弄不懂

» I'm sorry, You've lost me. Could you say it again?

很抱歉，你把我搞迷糊了。請你再講一遍。

» I'm lost.

我聽不懂。

＊ 這句話，用在你聽不懂，對方跟你解釋的話或教你的話時。

其它意思

» Hurry, there is no time to lose.

快一點，沒有時間浪費。

＊ lose 在這裡是「浪費」的意思。

» I lost my temper.

我發脾氣。

＊ lose 在這裡是「失去控制」的意思。

» We got lost in the big city.

我們在大城市裡迷了路。

＊ lose 在這裡是「迷路」的意思。

慣用語特好用

lose by

- Our team lost by ten points.
  我們隊輸了十分。

lose one's temper

- I'm sorry that I lost my temper.
  很抱歉，我發脾氣。

認為

» I don't **think** it's right.
我不認為那是對的。

» I don't **think** John is f i t for the job.
我不認為約翰適合這個工作。

» Do you **think** this car can last on such a long trip?
你認為這部車子可以跑這麼一趟旅程嗎？

» I **think** I'll go to Europe this summer.
我想我今年夏天會去歐洲。

» Do you **think** I should buy this book?
你認為我應該買這本書嗎？

» Who do you **think** will win?
你認為誰會贏？

思考

» You must think very carefully.
你必須小心的考慮。

想到

» I had never thought of becoming an actor.
我從未想過要當演員。

» I can't think where I left my keys.
我想不起來我把鑰匙放在哪裡。
＊ think 後面接疑問詞，表示「想不起來」的意思。

» I'm trying to think of someone who can take you to the airport.
我在想，有誰能載你去機場。

看重

» I know your boss thinks very highly of you.
我知道你的老闆很看重你。

» I think very highly of Mary's integrity.
我很敬重瑪莉的正直。

48

pay

付錢

» Let's each pay our own way.
我們各付各的。

» He paid his own way through college.
他自己賺錢完成大學學業。

» May I pay by credit card?
我可以用信用卡付帳嗎？

» I'll pay cash.
我要付現金。

» John paid some kids to wash the car.
他付錢給一些小孩子幫他洗車。

» I paid her $50 for the book.
我以五十元跟她買了這本書。

» Have you paid the phone bill yet?
你電話費繳了沒有？

» How much do they pay you?
他們付你多少錢？
＊ pay 在這裡是「付工資、薪水」的意思。

慣用語特好用

pay attention to

• I'm sorry. I wasn't paying attention to what you were saying.
對不起，我沒有注意聽你在說什麼。

>>> 49 <<<

fall

掉落

» The leaves have started falling again.
樹葉又開始掉了。

» Apples fell from the tree.
蘋果從樹上掉下來。

» Mary fell down the stairs and broke her leg.
瑪莉從樓梯跌下，摔斷了腿。

» He fell into a lake.
他掉進湖裡。

» The weather report says snow will fall tonight.

氣象報告説今晚會下雪。

跌倒

» She fell and hit her head.
她跌倒，碰到頭。

» She fell off the bike and broke her arm.
她從腳踏車上跌下來，摔斷手臂。

溫度、價格等下跌；風勢、聲音等變弱

» In winter the temperature often falls below zero.
冬天時，氣溫常降到零下。

» Interest rates fell sharply.
利息突然下降。

» House prices are falling.
屋價在下跌。

>>>

» The price of gas has fallen by one dollar.

油價已經下跌一塊錢。

» The storm fell towards evening.

近黃昏時，暴風雨的勢頭減弱了。

其它的用法

» The government fell and was replaced by another.

這個政府垮台，被其它人取代。

* fall 在這裡是「政府垮台」的意思。

» The city fell after a long battle.

在久戰之後，該城市被攻破。

* fall 在這裡是「城市、陣地被攻破」的意思。

» The accent falls on the second syllable.

重音落在第二音節。

* fall 在這句話裡是「落在」的意思。

慣用語特好用

fall asleep

- I fell asleep while watching the movie.
  我看電影時睡著了。

fall apart

- The club I belonged to fell apart.
  我參加的社團散了。

fall in love with

- John fell in love with Mary, but she only wanted to be friends.
  約翰愛上瑪莉，但是她只想作普通朋友。

fall off something

- John fell off the bike and broke his arm.
  約翰從腳踏車上摔下來，摔斷手臂。

50 cut

切

» The birthday girl is **cutting** the cake.

壽星在切蛋糕了。

» Can you **cut** another slice for me, please?

你可以再切一塊給我嗎？

＊這句話用在，你要對方再切一片時，這裡可能是你要對方切蛋糕、水果、麵包、一塊肉等。

剪頭髮

» Where do you have your hair **cut**?

你都在哪裡剪頭髮？

» You should have your hair **cut** already.

你應該剪頭髮了？

割傷

» John cut his chin when he shaved.

約翰刮鬍子的時候，割傷他的下巴。

減低

» The company will lay off two hundred people to cut the cost.

公司要裁員兩百人，以減低開銷。

» His salary was cut by 20%.

他被減薪百分之二十。

慣用語特好用

cut class

- If Mary keeps cutting classes, she'll fail the course.

  如果瑪莉繼續蹺課的話，她那一科一定會不及格。

cut corners

- Don't cut corners. Let's do the job right.

  不要偷工減料。我們把事情做好。

cut down on

- The doctor told John to cut down on Coke.

  醫生要約翰少喝可樂。

  * cut down on 某樣東西，就是「減少使用某樣東西」或「減少吃某樣東西」的意思。

口語特常說

Cut it out.

Cut it out. 這句口語是用在，當你要叫對方，不要做他們現在正在做的事情時。例如：你的兩個朋友為了一件不重要的事情在爭辯不停，你覺得這件事情沒什麼好爭的，而且他們的爭吵也吵到你，你要他們別再爭了，你就可以跟他們說，Cut it out.。

打開

» Could you open the door for me?
你可以替我開門嗎？

» I'll open a bottle of champagne to celebrate your promotion.
我開一瓶香檳來慶祝你升遷。

» She opened the envelope and read the letter.
她打開信封看信。

» She opened the newspaper on the table.
她翻開桌上的報紙。

» He opened his arms and welcomed us.

他張開雙臂歡迎我們。

開始營業

» What time does your store open?

你們商店什麼時候開？

新開張

» They are opening a new supermarket.

有一家新的超級市場要開張。

開始

» He opened his speech with a joke.

他以笑話開始他的演說。

開花

» The roses are starting to open.

玫瑰花開始開花。

停留；逗留

» Can you **stay** for dinner?
你可以留下來吃晚飯嗎？

» I can't **stay** long. I'll have to leave soon.
我不能留太久。我很快就要走。

» She **stayed** at the office and worked late.
她留在辦公室裡，工作到很晚。

保持某一狀況

» The weather **stayed** bad all day.
一整天天氣都很不好。

» The unemployment rate **stayed** below

three percent.

失業率保持在 3% 以下。

» I'm the only one who stayed sober at the party.

我是宴會中唯一保持清醒的人。

» Stay away from my computer.

別碰我的電腦。

居留；暫住

» My parents are staying with us for a few days.

我的父母要在我家住幾天。

» She was staying in the same hotel as I.

她跟我住同一個旅館。

» How long will you stay here?

你要在這裡住多久？

慣用語特好用

stay up

- If I stay up, I'm sleepy the next day.
  如果我熬夜，隔天我會想睡覺。
- I can't stay up that late.
  我不能熬到那麼晚。

stay over

- Can I stay over at Mary's tonight?
  我可以在瑪莉家過夜嗎？
  ＊stay over 就是「在別人家過夜」的意思。

口語特常說

stay put

叫對方 stay put，就是叫對方留在某一個地方別離開，例如：你要下車去買個東西，你叫對方留在車上別下來，整句話英語的説法就是 You stay put in the car while I run to the store.

好流利！用動詞溜英語

英語系列：46

作者／施孝昌
出版者／哈福企業有限公司
地址／新北市板橋區五權街16號
電話／(02) 2945-6285　傳真／(02) 2945-6986
郵政劃撥／31598840　戶名／哈福企業有限公司
出版日期／2018年2月　再版二刷／2018年8月
定價／NT$ 299元 (附MP3)

全球華文國際市場總代理／采舍國際有限公司
地址／新北市中和區中山路2段366巷10號3樓
電話／(02) 8245-8786　傳真／(02) 8245-8718
網址／www.silkbook.com 新絲路華文網

香港澳門總經銷／和平圖書有限公司
地址／香港柴灣嘉業街12號百樂門大廈17樓
電話／(852) 2804-6687　傳真／(852) 2804-6409
定價／港幣100元 (附MP3)

圖片／shuttlestock
email／haanet68@Gmail.com
網址／Haa-net.com
facebook／Haa-net 哈福網路商城

國家圖書館出版品預行編目資料

好流利！用動詞溜英語 / 施孝昌著. --
新北市：哈福企業, 2018.02
面；　公分. -- (英語系列；46)

ISBN 978-986-94966-8-1(平裝附光碟片)
1.英語 2.詞彙 3.會話

805.12　　107001222